Hell no. It can't be.

Darius King tightened his fingers on the champagne flute in his hand, the fragile stem in danger of snapping.

Shock and disbelief blasted him like the frigid winds of a Chicago winter storm, freezing him in place. Motionless, he stared at the petite brunette across the ballroom as she smiled at a waiter and accepted her own glass of wine. Though he'd only met her a couple of times, he recognized that smile. Remembered the same tinges of shyness in it. Remembered the lush, sensual curves of the mouth that belied that hint of coy innocence.

Isobel Hughes.

Not Wells. He refused to honor her with the last name she'd schemed and lied to win, then defiled for the two years she'd been married to his best friend. She didn't deserve to wear that name. Never had.

Rage roared through him at her gall, at the bold audacity it required to walk into this mansion as if she belonged here. As if she hadn't destroyed a man and dragged his grieving, ravaged family to the very brink of destruction themselves.

"What is she doing here?" Gabriella Wells gasped. "How did she even manage to get in?"

"I have no idea," he answered.

But he was about to find out.

* * *

The Billionaire's Bargain is part of the Blackout Billionaires trilogy from Naima Simone!

Dear Reader,

I'm so excited to be a part of the Harlequin Desire family and to bring you the Blackout Billionaires!

I remember watching a TV show where a blackout plunged a city into darkness. All the shenanigans that occurred had me thinking, *Wow*. What if a blackout happened, throwing couples together? What secrets would they share within the security of the dark? What inhibitions would they loosen? I had to find out!

In *The Billionaire's Bargain*, Darius King and Isobel Hughes aren't strangers. And when the light of day reveals their true identities, they are both... less than enthused. Isobel is the widow of Darius's best friend—the best friend he believes her faithlessness and cruelty drove to his death. But she's also the mother of his friend's son. And he'll put aside his animosity and bitterness toward her to care for the boy. Isobel, a survivor of a disastrous marriage, would do anything to provide for her son. Even become engaged to the enemy.

I hope you enjoy this story of family drama, secrets, forgiveness, passion and, most important, love. And remember, what happens in the dark never stays in the dark.

Happy reading!

Naima Simone

NAIMA SIMONE

THE BILLIONAIRE'S BARGAIN

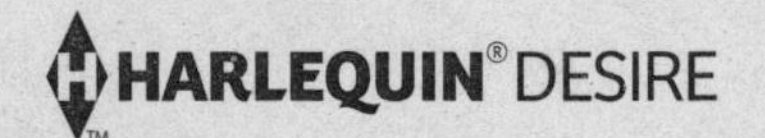

ISBN-13: 978-1-335-60370-8

The Billionaire's Bargain

This edition published by arrangement with Harlequin Books S.A.

For questions and comments about the quality of this book, please contact us at CustomerService@Harlequin.com.

Printed in U.S.A.

USA TODAY bestselling author **Naima Simone**'s love of romance was first stirred by Harlequin books pilfered from her grandmother. Now she spends her days writing sizzling romances with a touch of humor and snark.

She is wife to her own real-life superhero and mother to two awesome kids. They live in perfect, domestically challenged bliss in the Southern United States.

Harlequin Desire

Blackout Billionaires

The Billionaire's Bargain

Visit her Author Profile page at Harlequin.com, or naimasimone.com, for more titles.

You can find Naima Simone on Facebook, along with other Harlequin Desire authors, at Facebook.com/harlequindesireauthors!

To Gary. 143.

One

Delilah. Jezebel. Yoko. Monica.

According to past and recent history, they were all women who'd supposedly brought down a powerful man. Isobel Hughes silently snorted. Many of the people inside this North Shore mansion would include her name on that tarnished list.

Swallowing a sigh, she started up the stairs of the pillared mansion that wouldn't be out of place in the French countryside. Sitting on acres of meticulously landscaped grounds, the structure screamed decadence and obscene wealth. And though only a couple of hours' travel separated it from her tiny South Deering apartment, those minutes and miles might as well be years and states.

I can do this. I have no choice *but to do this.*

Quietly dragging in another deep breath, she paused as the tall, wide stained-glass doors opened to reveal an imposing gentleman dressed in black formal wear. His tuxedo might fit him perfectly, but Isobel didn't mistake him for who, or what, he was: security.

Security to protect the rarefied elite of Chicago high society and keep the riffraff out of the Du Sable City Gala.

Nerves tumbled and jostled inside her stomach like exes battling it out. Because she was a member of the riffraff who would be booted out on her common ass if she were discovered.

Fixing a polite but aloof mask on her face, she placed the expected invitation into the guard's outstretched hand as if it were a Golden Ticket. As he inspected the thick ivory paper with its gold engraved wording, she held her breath and resisted the urge to swipe her damp palms down the floor-length black gown she'd found at a consignment shop. Once upon a time, that invitation would've been authentic. But that had been when she'd been married to Gage Wells, golden child of the Wells family, one of Chicago's oldest and wealthiest lineages. When she'd believed Gage had been her handsome prince, the man who loved her as much as she'd adored him. Before she'd realized her prince was worse than a frog—he was a snake with a forked tongue.

She briefly closed her eyes. The present needed all of her focus. And with Gage dead these past two years and her exiled from the social circle she'd never belonged in, the present required that she resort to deception. Her brother's highly illegal skills were usually employed for forged IDs such as driver's licenses, birth certificates and passports for the city's more criminal element, not counterfeit invites to Chicago's balls. But he'd come through, and as the security guard scanned the invitation and waved a hand in front of him, she whispered a thanks to her brother.

The music that had sounded subdued outside seemed to fill the space here. Whimsical notes of flutes and powerful, bright chords of violins reverberated off the white marble walls. Gold tiles graced the floor, ebbing out in the shape of a flowering lotus, and a huge crystal-and-gold chandelier suspended from the glass ceiling seemed to be a delicate waterfall over that bloom. Two sets of staircases with gilded, intricate railings curved away from the walls and ascended to the next level of the home.

And she was stalling. Ogling her surroundings only delayed the inevitable.

And the inevitable awaited her down the hall, where music and chatter and laughter drifted. All too soon, she approached the wide entrance to the ballroom, and the glass doors opened wide in invitation.

But instead of feeling welcomed, nausea roiled and shuddered in her belly.

You can still turn around and leave. It's not too late.

The tiny whisper inside her head offered a lifeline she desperately wanted to grasp.

But then an image of her son wavered across her mind's eye, invoking an overwhelming swell of love. The thought of Aiden never failed to grasp her heart and squeeze it. He was a gift—*her* gift. And she would do anything—suffer anything—for him.

Including seeking out her dead husband's family and throwing her pride at the feet of the people who despised her. She'd committed the cardinal sins of being poor and falling for their golden child.

Well, she'd paid for that transgression. In spades.

Over the last couple of years, she'd reached out to her husband's family through email and old-fashioned snail mail, sending them pictures of Aiden, offering updates. But every email bounced back, and every letter was returned to the sender. They hadn't wanted anything to do with her or with the beautiful boy they considered her bastard.

She wanted nothing more than to forget their existence, just as they'd wiped hers out of their minds. But to keep a roof over Aiden's head, to ensure he didn't have to shiver in the increasingly chilly October nights or go to sleep hungry as she debated which overdue bill to pay, she would risk the wrath and derision of the Wells family.

The mental picture of her baby when she'd left him tonight—safe and happy with her mom—extinguished her flare of panic. Because it wouldn't do to enter these doors scared. The guests in this home would sense that weakness. And like sharks with bloody chum, they would circle and attack. Devour.

Inhaling yet another deep breath, she moved forward. Armored herself with pride. Ready to do battle.

Because she could never forget. This was indeed a battle.

One she couldn't afford to lose.

* * *

Hell no. It can't be.

Darius King tightened his fingers on the champagne flute in his hand, the fragile stem in danger of snapping.

Shock and disbelief blasted him like the frigid winds of a Chicago winter storm, freezing him in place. Motionless, he stared at the petite brunette across the ballroom as she smiled at a waiter and accepted her own glass of wine. Though he'd only met her a couple of times, he recognized that smile. Remembered the shyness in it. Remembered the lush, sensual curve of the mouth that belied that hint of coy innocence.

Isobel fucking Hughes.

Not Wells. He refused to honor her with the last name she'd schemed and lied to win, then defiled for the two years she'd been married to his best friend. She didn't deserve to wear that name. Never had.

Rage roared through him, incinerating the astonishment that had paralyzed him. Only fury remained. Fury at her gall. Fury at the bold audacity it required to walk into this mansion as if she belonged here. As if she hadn't destroyed a man and dragged his grieving, ravaged family to the very brink of destruction.

"Oh, my God." Beside him, Gabriella Wells gasped, her fingers curling around his biceps and digging deep. "Is that..."

"Yes," Darius growled, unable to soften his tone for Gage's sister, whom he cared for as if she were his own sibling. "It's her."

"What is she doing here?" Gabriella snarled, the

same anger that had gripped him darkening her lovely features. "How did she even manage to get in?"

"I have no idea."

But he'd find out. And asses would be kicked when he did. The security here was supposed to be tighter than that of the goddamn royal family's, considering the people in attendance: politicians, philanthropists, celebrities, the country's wealthiest business people. Yet evidence that the security team wasn't worth shit stood in this very room, sipping champagne.

"How could she dare show her face here? Hell, *in Chicago*?" Gabriella snapped. "I thought we were rid of her when she left for California. No doubt whatever sucker she attached herself to finally got tired of her and kicked the gold-digging bitch out. And she's probably here to suck Dad and Mother dry. I swear to God…" She didn't finish the thought, but charged forward, her intentions clear.

"No." He encircled her arm, his hold gentle but firm. Gabriella halted, shooting him a let-me-go-now-dammit glance over her shoulder. Fire lit the emerald gaze that reminded him so much of Gage's. At twenty-four, she was six years younger than her older brother, and had adored him. And though she'd been in college, studying abroad for most of her brother's marriage, tales of her sister-in-law had reached her all the way in England, and Gabriella despised the woman who'd hurt Gage so badly.

Darius shook his head in reply to her unspoken demand of freedom. "No," he repeated. "We're not causing a scene. And running over there and confronting her will do just that. Think of your parents, Gabriella," he murmured.

The anger didn't bleed from her expression at the reminder, but concern banked the flames in her eyes to a simmer, and the thin, grim line of her mouth softened. Neither of them needed to voice the worry that Darius harbored. Gabriella and Gage's father, Baron Wells, had suffered a heart attack the previous year. Nothing could convince Darius that it hadn't been grief over his son's death in a sudden car accident that had precipitated the attack, added to long work hours, poor eating habits and a lax exercise regimen.

The last several months had finally seen the return of the imposing, dignified man Darius had known and admired all of his life. Still, a sense of fragility stubbornly clung to Baron. A fragility Darius feared could escalate into something more threatening if Baron glimpsed his dead son's widow.

"I'll go and find security so they can escort her out," he said, the calm in his voice a mockery of the rage damn near consuming him. "You can locate your parents to make sure they don't realize what's going on."

Yes, he'd have Isobel Hughes thrown out, but not before he had a few words with her. The deceitful, traitorous woman should've counted herself lucky that he hadn't come after her when she'd skipped town two years ago. But with the Wells family shattered over their son and brother's death, they'd been his first priority. And as long as Isobel had remained gone, they didn't have to suffer a daily reminder of the woman who'd destroyed Gage with her manipulations and faithlessness. In spite of the need to mete out his own brand of justice, Darius had allowed her to disappear with the baby the Wells family doubted was their grandson and nephew. But now…

Now she'd reappeared, and all bets were off.

She'd thrown down the gauntlet, and fuck if he wouldn't enjoy snatching it up.

"Okay," Gabriella agreed, enclosing his hand in hers and squeezing. "Darius," she whispered. He tore his attention away from Isobel and transferred it to Gabriella. "Thank you for…" She swallowed. "Thank you," she breathed.

"No need for any of that," he replied, brushing a kiss over the top of her black curls. "Family. We always take care of one another."

She nodded, then turned and disappeared into the throng of people.

Anticipation hummed beneath his skin as he moved forward. Several people slowed his progress for meaningless chatter, but he didn't deter from his path. He tracked her, noting that she'd moved from just in side the entrance to one of the floor-to-ceiling glass doors that led to a balcony. Good. The only exit led out onto that balcony, and the temperature of the October night had probably dropped even more since he'd arrived. She wouldn't venture through those doors and into the cold. He had a location to give security.

It was unfair that a woman who possessed zero morals and conscience should exhibit none of it on her face or her body. But then, if her smooth, golden skin or slender-but-curvaceous body did reveal any of her true self, she wouldn't be able to snare men in her silken web.

Long, thick, dark brown hair that gleamed with hints of auburn fire under the chandelier's light flowed over one slim shoulder and a just-less-than-a-handful breast. Dispassionately, he scanned her petite frame. The strapless, floor-length black gown clung to her, lifting her full curves so a hint of shadowed cleavage teased, promised. A waist that a man—not him—could span with his hands flowed into rounded hips and a tight, worship-worthy ass that he didn't need to see to remember. Even when he'd first met her—as the only witness and friend at her and Gage's quickie courthouse marriage—it'd amazed him how such a small woman could possess curves so dangerous they should come with a blaring warning sign. Back then he'd appreciated her curves. Now he despised them for what they truly were—an enticing lure to trap unsuspecting game.

Dragging his inspection up the siren call of her body, he took in the delicate bones that provided the structure for an almost elfin face. One of his guilty pleasures was fantasy novels and movies. Tolkien, Martin, Rowling, King. And he could easily imagine Arwen, half-Elven daughter of King Elrond in *The Lord of the Rings*, resembling Isobel. Beautiful. Ethereal. Though he couldn't catch the color of her eyes from this distance, he clearly recalled their striking color. A vivid and startling blue-gray that only enhanced the impression of otherworldly fragility. But then there was her mouth. It splintered her air of innocence. The shade-too-wide lips with their full, plump curves called to mind ragged, hoarse groans in the darkest part of night. Yeah, those lips could cause a man's cock to throb.

He ground his teeth together, the minute flare of pain along his jaw grounding him. It didn't ease the stab of guilt over the sudden, unexpected clench of lust in his gut. He could hate himself for that gut-punch of desire. Didn't he, more than anyone, know that a pretty face could hide the black, empty hole where a heart should be? Could conceal the blackest of souls? His own ex-wife had taught him that lesson, and he'd received straight fucking A's. Yeah, his dick might be slow on the uptake, but his head—the one that ruled him, contrary to popular opinion about men—possessed full disclosure and was fully aware.

Isobel Hughes was one of those pretty faces.

As if she'd overheard her name in his head, Isobel lifted her chin and surveyed the crowded ballroom. Probably searching for Baron and Helena. If she thought he'd allow her within breathing space of Gage's parents, she'd obviously been smoking too much of that legalized California weed. He'd do anything to protect them; he'd failed to protect Gage, and that knowledge gnawed at him, an open wound that hadn't healed in two years. No way in hell would this woman have another shot at the people he loved. At his family.

The thought propelled him forward. Time to end this and escort her back to whatever hole she'd crawled out of.

Clenching his jaw, he worked his way to the ballroom entrance. Several minutes later, he waited in one of the side hallways for the head of security. Glancing down at his watch, he frowned. The man should've arrived already…

Darkness.

Utter darkness.

Dimly, Darius caught the sound of startled cries and shouts, but the deafening pounding of his heart muted most of the fearful noise.

He stumbled backward, and his spine smacked the wall behind him. Barely able to draw a breath into his constricted lungs, he frantically patted his jacket and then his pants pockets for his cell phone. Nothing. *Damn.* He must've left it in the car. He never left his phone. Never…

The thick blackness surrounded him. Squeezed him so that he jerked at his bow tie, clawing at material that seconds ago had been perfectly comfortable.

Air.

He needed air.

But all he inhaled, all he swallowed, was more of the obsidian viscosity that clogged his nostrils, throat and chest.

In the space of seconds, his worst, most brutal nightmare had come to life.

He was trapped in the dark.

Alone.

And he was drowning in it.

Two

Blackout.

Malfunction. Doors locked.

Remain calm.

The words shouted in anything but calm voices outside the bathroom door bombarded Isobel. Perched on the settee in the outer room of the ladies' restroom, she hunched over her cell phone, which had only 2 percent battery life left.

"C'mon," she ordered her fingers to cooperate as she fumbled over the text keyboard. In her nerves, she kept misspelling words, and *damn autocorrect*, it kept "fixing" the words that were actually right. Finally she finished her message and hit send.

Mom, is everything okay? How is Aiden?

Fingers clutching the little burner phone, she—not for the first time—wished she could afford a regular cell. But with her other responsibilities, that bill had been one of the first things she'd cut. Constantly buying minutes and battling a battery that didn't hold a charge presented a hassle, but the prepaid phone did the job. After seconds that seemed like hours, a message popped up on the screen.

He's fine, honey. Sleeping. We're all good. Stay put. It's a blackout and we've been advised to remain inside. I love you and take care of yourself.

Relief washed over Isobel in a deluge. If she hadn't already been sitting down, she would've sunk to the floor. For the first time since the world had plunged into darkness, she could breathe.

After several moments, she located the flashlight app and aimed it in the direction of where she believed the door to be. The deep blackness seemed to swallow up the light, but she spied the handle and sighed. Without ventilation, the area was growing stuffy. The hallway had to be better. At the very least, she wouldn't feel like the walls were closing in on her. Claustrophobia had never been a problem for her, but this was enough to have anyone on edge.

She grabbed the handle and pulled the door open, the weak beam illuminating the floor only feet in front of her. As soon as she stepped out into the hall, the light winked, then disappeared.

"No, not yet," she muttered, flipping the phone over. But, nope, the cell had died. "Dammit."

Frustration and not-a-little fear scrabbled up her chest, lodging there. Inhaling a deep breath and holding it, she forced herself to calm down. Okay. One thing her two years in Los Angeles had granted her was a sense of direction. The ballroom lay to the left. Follow the wall until it gave way to the small alcove and the side entrance she'd exited.

No problem. She could do this.

Probably.

Maybe.

Releasing that same gulp of air, she shuffled forward, hands groping until they knocked against the wall. Step one down.

With halting steps, she slid along, palms flattened, skimming. The adjacent corridor shouldn't be too far…

Her chest bumped into a solid object seconds after her hands collided with it. A person. A big person, if the width of the shoulders and chest under her fingers were anything to go by.

"Oh, God. I'm sorry." She snatched her arms back. Heat soared up her neck and poured into her face. She'd just felt up a man in the dark.

Horrified, she shifted backward, but her heel caught on the hem of her dress, and she pitched forward. Slamming against that same hard expanse of muscles she'd just molested. "*Dammit*. I—"

The second apology drifted away as a hoarse, ragged sound penetrated the darkness and reached her ears. For a long moment, she froze, her hands splayed wide over the stranger's chest. It rapidly rose and fell, the pace unnatural. She jerked her head up, staring into the space where his face should've been. But she didn't need to glimpse his features to understand this man suffered some kind of distress. Because those rough, serrated, *wounded* sounds originated from him.

The urge to comfort, to stop those god-awful moans overrode all embarrassment at having touched him without his permission. At this moment, she needed to touch him. To ease his pain.

As she slid one palm over his jackhammering heart, she swept the other over his shoulder and down his arm until she enclosed his long fingers in hers. Then she murmured, "Hi. Talk about an awkward meet cute, right? Citywide blackout. Get felt up in the hallway. Sounds like the beginning of a rom-com starring Ryan Reynolds."

The man didn't reply, and his breathing continued to sough out of his lungs, but his fingers curled around hers, clutching them tight. As if she were his lifeline.

Relief and determination to tow him away from whatever tormented him swelled within her. It didn't require a PhD in psychology to figure out that this man was in the throes of a panic attack. But she had zero experience with how to handle that situation. Still, he'd responded to her voice, her presence. So she'd continue talking.

"Do you know who Ryan Reynolds is?" She didn't wait for his answer but kept babbling. "*The Green Lantern*? *Deadpool*? I'm leading with those movies, because if you're anything like my brother, if I'd have said *The Proposal*, you would've stared at me like I'd suddenly started speaking Mandarin. Well…that is, if you *could* stare at me right now." She snickered. "What I wouldn't give for Riddick's eyes right now. To be able to see in the dark? Although you could keep Slam City and, ya know, the murder. Have you ever seen *Pitch Black* or *The Chronicles of Riddick*?"

This time she received a squeeze of her fingers and a slight change in the coarseness of his breathing. A grin curved her lips. Good. That had to be a positive sign, right?

"*The Chronicles of Riddick*? I enjoyed watching Vin Diesel for two hours, but the movie? Meh. *Pitch Black*, though, was amazing. One of the best sci-fi movies ever. Only beat out by *Aliens* and *The Matrix*. Although I still maintain that *The Matrix Revolutions* never happened, just as *Dirty Dancing 2* is a dirty rumor. They're like Voldemort. Those Movies That Shall Not Be Named."

A soft, shaky chuckle drifted above her, but seemed to echo in the dark, empty hallway like a sonic boom. Probably because she'd been aching to hear it. Not that she'd been aware of that need until this moment.

An answering laugh bubbled up inside her, but she shoved it back down, opting to continue with what had been working so far. Talking. The irony that this was the longest conversation she'd indulged in with a person outside of her family in two years wasn't lost on her. Cruel experience had taught her to be wary of strangers, especially those with pretty faces wielding charm like a Highlander's claymore. The last time she'd trusted a beautiful appearance, she'd ended up in a loveless, controlling, soul-stealing sham of a marriage.

But in the dark…

In the dark lived a kind of freedom where she could lose her usual restrictions, step out of the protective box she'd created for her life. Because here, she couldn't see this man, and he couldn't see her. There was no judgment. If he were attending the Du Sable City Gala, then that meant he most likely came from wealth—the kind of wealth that had once trapped her in a gilded prison. Yet in this corridor in the middle of a blackout, money, status, lineage traced back to the Mayflower—none of that mattered. Here, they were only two people holding on to each other to make it through.

"My next favorite sci-fi is *Avatar.* Which is kind of funny, considering the famous line from the movie is 'I see you.'" She couldn't smother her laughter. And didn't regret the display of amusement when it garnered another squeeze of her hand. "Do you have a favorite?"

She held her breath, waiting. Part of her waited to see if his panic attack had finally passed. But the other part of her wanted—no, *needed*—to hear his voice. That part wondered if it would match his build.

Being tucked away in a mansion's dark hallway in a blackout…the insane circumstances had to be the cause of her desire. Because it'd been years since she'd been curious about anything regarding a man.

"*The Terminator.*"

Oh. Wow. That voice. Darker than the obsidian blanket that draped the city. Deeper than the depths of the ocean she sorely missed. Sin wrapped in the velvet embrace of sweet promise.

A dangerous voice.

One that invited a person to commit acts that might shame them in the light of day, acts a person would revel in during the secretive, shadowed hours of night.

Her eyes fluttered closed, and her lips parted, as if she could breathe in that slightly abraded yet smooth tone. As if she could taste it.

As if she could taste him.

What the hell?

The inane thought rebounded against the walls of her skull, and she couldn't evict it. Her eyes flew open, and she stared wide into nothing. For the second time that evening, she thanked God. At this moment, she offered her gratitude because she couldn't be seen. That no one had witnessed her unprecedented, humiliating reaction to a man's *voice*.

"A classic." She struggled to recapture and keep hold of the light, teasing note she'd employed with him BTV. Before The Voice. "But I take your *Terminator* and one-up you with *Predator*."

A scoff. "That wasn't sci-fi."

Isobel frowned even though he couldn't see her disapproval. "Are you kidding me?" She dropped her hand from his chest and jammed it on her hip. "Hello? There was a big-ass alien in it. How is that not sci-fi?"

A snort this time. "It's horror. Using your logic would mean *Avatar* was a romance."

Okay, so this guy might have the voice of a fallen

angel tempting her to sin, but his movie knowledge sucked.

"I think I liked you better when you weren't talking," she grumbled.

She was rewarded with a loud bark of laughter that did the impossible. Made his voice even sexier. Desire slid through her veins in a slow, heady glide.

She stiffened. No. Impossible. It'd been years since she'd felt even the slightest flicker of this thing that heated her from the inside out.

If she harbored even the tiniest shred of common sense, she'd back away from this man now and blind-man's bluff it until she placed some much needed distance between them. Desire had once fooled her into falling in love. And falling in love had led to a heartbreaking betrayal she was still recovering from.

No, she should make sure he was okay, then leave. With moving back to Chicago, raising her son as a single mother and working a full-time job, she didn't have the time or inclination for something as mercurial as desire.

You're sitting here in the dark with him, not dating him.

One night. Just one night.

She sighed.

And stayed.

"Is something wrong?" A large hand settled on her shoulder and cupped it. She gritted her teeth, refusing to lean into that gentle but firm hold.

"Nothing. Just these shoes," she lied, bending and

slipping off one and then the other to validate the fib. "They're beautiful, but hell on the feet."

He released another of those soft chuckles that sent her belly into a series of tumbles.

"What's your name?" His thumb stroked a lazy back-and-forth caress over her bare skin, and she sank her teeth into her bottom lip. Heat radiated from his touch. Until this moment, she hadn't known her shoulder was an erogenous zone. Funny the things she was finding out in the dark.

What had he asked? Right. Her name.

Alarm and dread filtered into her pleasure, tainting it. Gage had done a damn good job of demonizing her to his family, and then his family had made sure everyone with a willing ear and flapping gums knew Isobel as a lying, greedy whore. It'd been two years since she'd left Chicago, but the insular ranks of high society never forgot names when it came to scandals.

Again, she squeezed her eyes shut as if she could block out the scorn and derision that had once flayed her soul. She still yearned to be known as more than the cheap little gold digger people believed her to be.

"Why do you want my name?" she finally replied.

A short, but weighty pause. "Because I need to know who to thank," he murmured. "And considering we've known each other all of ten minutes, 'sweetheart' seems a little forward."

"I don't mind 'sweetheart,'" she blurted out. His grasp on her shoulder tightened, and a swirl of need pooled low in her belly. "What I mean is we don't need names here. In the dark, we can be other people, different people, and I like the idea of that."

The bit of deception plucked at her conscience. Because she had no doubt that if he was familiar with her name, he would want nothing to do with her. And selfish though it might be, she'd rather him believe she was some coy debutante than the notorious Widow Wells.

That large hand slid over her shoulder, up her neck and cradled the back of her head. A sigh escaped her before she could contain it.

"Are you hiding, sweetheart?" he rumbled.

The question could have sounded inane since it seemed like the whole city was hunkered down, cloaked in darkness. But she understood what he asked. And the lack of light made it easier to be honest. At least in this.

"Yes," she breathed, and braced herself for his possible rejection.

"You're stiffening again." The hand surrounding hers squeezed lightly, a gesture of comfort. "Don't worry, your secrets are as safe with me as you are." He paused, his fingertips pressing into her scalp. "Just as I am with you."

Oh, God. That…vulnerable admission had no business burrowing beneath skin and bone to her heart. But it did.

"Keep your name, but, sweetheart—" he heaved a heavy sigh, and for an all-too-brief moment he pressed his forehead to hers "—thank you."

"I…" She swallowed, a shiver dancing down her spine. Whether in delight or warning, she couldn't tell.

Probably both. "You're welcome. Anyone would've done the same," she whispered.

Something sharp edged through his low chuckle. "That's where you're wrong. Most people would've kept going, only concerned with themselves. Or they would've taken advantage."

She didn't answer; she wanted to refute him but couldn't. Because the sad fact was, he'd spoken the truth. Once she'd been a naïve twenty-year-old who'd believed in the good in people, in the happily-ever-after peddled by fairy tales. Gage had been her drug. And the withdrawal from him had nearly crushed her into the piece of nothing he'd constantly told her she was without him.

Shaking her head to get him out of her mind, she bent down and swept her hands along the floor, seeking the purse she'd dropped. Her fingertips bumped the beaded clutch, and with a small sound of victory, she popped it open and withdrew the snack bar she'd stashed there before leaving her apartment. With a two-year-old, keeping snacks on hand was a case of survival. And though her son hadn't joined her at the gala, she'd tossed the snack in out of habit. Now she patted herself on the back for her foresight.

Unbidden, a smile curved her lips. If Aiden could see her, he would be holding out his chubby little hand, demanding his "eats."

She pinched the bridge of her nose, battling back the sting in her eyes. Obtaining help for her son had driven her to this mansion, and she'd failed. It would be easy to blame the blackout for her not locating and approaching the Wellses. But she couldn't deny the truth. She'd left the ballroom and headed to the restroom to convince herself not to leave. The plunge of the city into darkness had snatched the decision out of her hands, granting her a convenient reprieve from facing down the people who'd made it their lives' purpose to ensure she understood just how unworthy and hated she was.

But it was only that—a reprieve. Because when it came down to a choice between her pride and providing a stable environment for her son, there wasn't a choice.

When the blackout ended, she still had to face the Wellses.

"Did I lose you?" His softly rumbled question drew her from her desperate thoughts.

Clearing her throat, she settled on the floor, tucking her legs under her. She tugged on the hem of his pants, and he accepted her silent invitation, sinking down beside her. When the thick muscles of his leg brushed her knee, she reached out and skated a palm down his arm until she located his hand. She pressed half the cereal bar into it.

"What is this?" His low roll of rich laughter slid over her skin, and she involuntarily tightened her grip on her half.

"Dinner." Isobel bit into the snack and hummed. The oats, almonds and chocolate weren't caviar and toast points, but they did the job in a pinch. And this situation definitely qualified as a pinch.

"I have to say this is a first," he murmured, amusement still warming his voice.

God, she liked it. A lot. No matter how foolish that feeling might be.

"So, you don't want to share your name," he continued. "And I'll respect that. But since I'm sharing a cereal bar with you, I feel like I should know more about you besides your predilection for sci-fi movies. Tell me something about you."

She didn't immediately reply, instead nibbling on her snack while she figured out how to dodge his request. She didn't want to give him any details that might assist him in figuring out her identity. But another nebulous reason, one that she felt silly for even thinking, flitted through her head.

Giving him details about herself...pieces of herself... meant she couldn't get them back.

And she feared that. Had been taught to fear that.

Yet...

She bowed her head, silently cursing herself. What was it about this man? She'd never seen his face, didn't know his name. And still, he called to her in a way that electrified her. If she'd learned anything from the past, she would shield herself.

"I'm a grudge-holder," she said, the words escaping. *Damn it.* "I'll never let my brother off the hook for burning my Christmas Barbie's hair to the scalp when I was seven. I still give Elaine Lanier side-eye, whenever I see her, for making out with my boyfriend in the eleventh grade. And I will never, ever forgive Will Smith for *Wild, Wild West.*"

A loud bark of laughter echoed between them, and she grinned. The sound warmed her like the sun's beams.

She tapped his leg. A mistake on her part. As she settled her hand back in her lap, she could still feel the strength of his muscle against her fingertips. Good God. The man was *hard.* She rubbed her fingertips against her leg as if she could erase the sensation. “Now your turn,” she said, forcing a teasing note into her voice. “Tell me something about yourself.”

He hesitated, and for a moment, she didn’t think he would answer, but then he shifted beside her, and his thigh pressed closer, harder against her knee. Her breath snagged in her throat. Heat pulsed through her from that point of contact, and she savored it. For the first time in years, she…embraced it.

“I love to fish,” he finally murmured. “Not deep sea or competitive fishing. Just sitting on a dock with a rod, barefoot, sun beating down on you, surrounded by quiet. Interrupted only by the gently lapping water. We would vacation at our summer home in Hilton Head, and my father and I would spend hours at the lake and dock behind the house. We’d talk or just enjoy the silence and each other. We even caught fish sometimes.”

His low chuckle contained humor, but also a hint of sadness. Her heart clenched at the possible reason why.

“Those were some of my best memories, and I still try to visit Hilton Head at least once a year, although I haven’t been in the last two…”

His voice trailed off, and unable to resist, she reached out, found his hand and wrapped her fingers around his, squeezing. Her heart thumped against her chest when his fingers tightened in response.

“I have the hugest crush on Dr. Phil. He’s so sexy.”

He snorted. "I cook the best eggplant parmesan you'll ever taste in your life. It's an existential experience."

Isobel snickered. "I can write with my toes. I can also eat, brush my teeth and play 'Heart and Soul' on the piano with them."

A beat of silence passed between them. "You do know I recognize that's from *The Breakfast Club*, right?"

Laughter burst from her, and she fell back against the wall, clutching her stomach. Wow. She hadn't laughed this hard or this much in so long. It was… freeing. And felt so damn good. Until this moment, she hadn't realized how much she'd missed it.

At twenty, she'd met Gage, and within months, they'd married. She'd gone from being a college student who worked part-time to help pay her tuition to the wife of one of Chicago's wealthiest men. His family had disapproved of their marriage and threatened to cut him off. Initially, Gage hadn't seemed to care. They'd lived in a small one-bedroom apartment in the Ukrainian Village neighborhood of Chicago, and they'd been happy. Or at least she'd believed they had been.

Months into their marriage, the charming, affectionate man she'd wed had morphed into a spoiled, emotionally abusive man-child. Not until it'd been too late had she discovered that his fear of being without his family's money and acceptance had trumped any love he'd harbored for Isobel. Her life had become a living hell.

So the last time she'd laughed like this had been those first four months of her marriage.

A failed relationship, tarnished dreams, battered self-confidence and single motherhood had stolen the carefree from her life, but here, stuck in a mansion with a faceless man, she'd found it again. Even if only for an instant.

"Hey." Masculine fingers glanced over her knee. "You still with me?"

"Yes," she said, shaking her head. "I'm still here."

"Good." His hand dropped away, and she missed it. Insane, she knew. But she did. "It's your turn. Because you phoned it in with the last one."

"So, we're *really* not going to talk about how you know the dialogue to *The Breakfast Club*?" she drawled.

"Yes, we're going to ignore it. Your turn."

After chuckling at the emphatic reply, she continued, "Fine. Okay, I..."

Seconds, minutes or hours had passed—she couldn't tell in this slice of time that seemed to exist outside of reality. They could've been on another plane, where his delicious scent provided air, and his deep, melodic voice wrapped around her, a phantom embrace.

And his touch? His touch was gravity, anchoring him to her, and her to him. In some manner—fingers enclosing hers, a thigh pressed to hers, a palm cupping the nape of her neck—he never ceased touching her. Logic reasoned that he needed that lodestone in the blackness so he didn't surrender to another panic attack.

Yet the heated sweetness that slid through her veins belied reason. No, he wanted to touch her...and, God, did she want to be touched.

She'd convinced herself that she didn't need desire anymore. Didn't need the melting pleasure, the hot press of skin to skin, of limbs tangling, bodies straining together toward that perfect tumble over the edge into the abyss.

Yes, she missed all of it.

But in the end, those moments weren't worth the disillusionment and loneliness that inevitably followed.

Here, though, with this man she didn't know, she basked in the return of the need, of the sweet ache that sensitized and pebbled her skin, and teased places that had lain dormant for too long. Her nipples furled into tight points, pressing against her strapless bra and gown. Sinuous flames licked at her belly…and lower.

God, she was hungry.

"You've gone quiet on me again, sweetheart," he murmured, sweeping a caress over the back of her hand that he clasped in his. "Talk to me. I need to hear your beautiful voice."

Did he touch all women this easily? Was he always this affectionate? Or was it the darkness? Did he feel freer, too? Without the accountability of propriety?

Or is it me?

As soon as the traitorous and utterly foolish thought whispered through her head, she banished it. Yes, these were extraordinary circumstances, and she was grabbing this slice in time for herself, but never could she forget who she was. Because this man might not know her identity, but he still believed her to be someone she absolutely wasn't—wealthy, a socialite…a woman who belonged.

"Sweetheart?"

That endearment. She shivered. It ignited a curl of heat in her chest. It loosed a razor-tipped arrow at the same target. No one had ever called her "sweetheart." Or "baby" or any of those personal endearments. Gage used to call her Belle, shortening her name and because he'd met her in her regular haunt, the University of Illinois's library, like a modern-day version of the heroine from *Beauty and the Beast*. Later, the affectionate nickname had become a taunt, a criticism of her unsophisticated and naïve nature.

She hated that name now.

But every time this man called her sweetheart, she felt cherished, wanted. Even though it was also a stark reminder that he didn't know her name. That she was lying to him by omission.

"Can I ask you a question?" she blurted out.

"Isn't that kind of our MO?" he drawled. "Ask."

Now that she could satisfy the curiosity that had been gnawing at her since she'd first encountered him, she hesitated. She had no right—never mind it not being her business—to probe into his history and private pain. But as hypocritical as it made her, she sought a piece of him she sensed he wouldn't willingly offer someone else.

"Earlier, when I first bumped into you…you were having a panic attack," she began. He stiffened, tension turning his body into a replica of the marble statue adorning the fountain outside the mansion. Sitting so close to him, she swore she could feel icy waves emanate from him. Unease trickled through her. *Damn it.*

She should've left it alone. "I'm sorry…" she rasped, tugging on her hand, trying to withdraw it from his hold. "I shouldn't have pried."

But he didn't release her. Her heart stuttered as his grip on her strengthened.

"Don't," he ordered.

Don't what? Ask him any more questions? Pull away? How pathetic did it make her that she hoped it was the latter?

"You're the only thing keeping me sane," he admitted in a voice so low that, even in the blackness that magnified every sound, she barely caught the admission.

A thread of pain throbbed through his confession, and she couldn't resist the draw of it. Scooting closer until her thigh pressed against his, she lifted the hand not clasped in his to his hard chest. The drum of his heart vibrated against her palm, running up her arm and echoing in her own chest.

She felt and heard his heavy inhale. And she parted her lips, ready to tell him to forget it. To apologize again for intruding, but his big hand covered hers, halting her words.

"My parents died when I was sixteen."

"God," she breathed. That hint of sadness she'd detected earlier when he'd talked about fishing with his father… She'd suspected, and now he'd confirmed it. "I'm so sorry."

"Plane crash on their way back from a business meeting in Paris. Ordinarily my mother wouldn't have been with my father, but they decided to treat it as an anniversary trip. They were my foundation. And I…" He paused, and Isobel waited.

She couldn't imagine… Her father had been a non-factor in her life for most of her childhood, but her mom… Her mother had been her support system, her rock, even through the years with Isobel and Aiden's move to California and back. Losing her…she closed her eyes and leaned her head against his shoulder, offering whatever comfort he needed as he relayed the details of the tragedy that had scarred him.

"My best friend and his family took me in. I don't know what would've happened to me, where I would be now, without them. But at the time, I was lost. Adrift. In the months afterward, I'd skip school or leave my friend's house in the middle of the night to go to the building where we'd lived. The penthouse had been sold, so I no longer had access to my home, but I would sneak into the basement through a window. It had a loosened bar that I would remove and squeeze through. I'd sit there for hours, just content to be in the building, if not in the place where I'd lived with them. My best friend—he followed me one night when I sneaked out, so he knew about it. But he never told."

Another pause, and again she didn't disturb him. She wanted to hug that best friend for standing by the boy-now-man. She'd had girlfriends in the past, but none that would've—or could've, given their own family situations—taken her in as if she were family. This friend of his, he must've been special.

"About four months after my parents' death, I'd left school again and went to the basement. I'd had a rough night. Nightmares and no sleep. That's the only reason I can think of for me falling asleep in the basement that day. I don't know what woke me up. The noise? The heat?" His shoulder rose and fell in a shrug under her cheek. "Like I said, I don't know. But when I did, the room was pitch-black. I couldn't even see my hands in front of my face. I heard what sounded like twigs snapping. But underneath that, distant but growing louder, was this dull roar. Like engines revving in a closed garage. I'd never been in one before, but somehow I knew. The building was on fire, and I was trapped."

"No," she whispered, fingers curling against his chest.

"I couldn't move. Thick black smoke filled the basement, and I choked on it, couldn't breathe. I can't tell you how long I laid there, paralyzed by fear or weak from inhaling smoke, but I thought I was going to die. That room—it became my tomb. A dark, burning tomb. But then I heard someone shouting my name and saw the high beam of a flashlight. It was my friend. I found out later that he'd heard about the fire on the news, and when I hadn't shown up at his house after school, he'd guessed where I'd gone. The firemen had believed they'd cleared the entire building, but he'd forced them to go back in and search the basement. He should've stayed outside and let them come find me, but he'd barreled past them and entered with only his shirt over his face to battle the smoke, putting his life in danger. But if he hadn't… He saved my life that day."

"Oh, thank God." Sliding her hand from under his, she wrapped her arm around his waist, curving her body into his. She'd known him for mere hours, and yet the thought of him dying, of being consumed by flames? It bothered her in a way that made no sense. "He was a hero."

"Yes, he was," he said softly. "He was a good man."

Was a good man. No. It couldn't be… Horror and disbelief crowded up her throat. "He's gone, too?"

"A couple of years now, but sometimes it seems like yesterday."

"I'm so sorry." Isobel shifted until she knelt beside him. She stroked her hand up his torso, searching out his face. Once she brushed over his hard, faintly stubbled jaw, she cupped it and lowered her head, until her forehead met his temple.

His fingers drifted over her cheek, and after a moment's hesitation, tunneled into her hair. Her lungs seized, shock infiltrating every vein, organ and limb. Only her heart seemed capable of movement, and it threw itself against her sternum, like an animal desperate for freedom from its cage.

Blunt fingertips dragged over her scalp. A moan clawed its way up her throat at the scratch and tug of her hair, but she trapped the sound behind clenched teeth. She couldn't prevent the shudder that worked its way through her. Not when it'd been *so long* since she'd been touched. Since pleasure had even been a factor. So. Long.

"I need to hear that lovely voice, sweetheart," he rumbled, turning and bowing his head so his lips grazed the column of her throat as he spoke. Sparks snapped under her skin as if her nerve endings had transformed into firecrackers, and his mouth was the lighter. "There are things I want to do to your mouth that require your permission."

"Like what?" Had she really just asked that question? And in that breathy tone? What was he doing to her?

Giving you what you're craving. Be brave and find out, her subconscious replied.

"Find out if it's as sweet as you are. Taste you. Savor you. Learn you," he murmured, answering her question. He untangled their clasped fingers and with unerring accuracy, located her chin and pinched it. Cool but soft strands of hair tickled her jaw, and then her cheek, as he lifted his head. Then warm gusts of air bathed her lips. She could taste him, his breath. Something potent with faint hints of lemon, like the champagne from earlier. But also, underneath, lay a darker, enigmatic flavor. Him. She didn't need to pinpoint its origin to know it was all him. "Then I want to take your mouth. Want you to take mine."

"I…" Desperate, aching need robbed her of words. Of thought.

"Give me the words, sweetheart." He didn't breach that scant inch of space between them, waiting on her consent, her permission.

When so much had been ripped from her in the past, choices not even offered, that seeking of her agreement squeezed her heart even as his words caused a spasm to roll through her sex.

"Yes," she said. Then, as if confirming to herself that she was indeed breaking her self-imposed rules about caution and recklessness, she whispered again, "Yes."

With a growl, he claimed that distance.

She expected him to crush his mouth to hers, to conquer her like a wild storm leveling everything in its path. And she would've thrown herself into the whirlwind, been willingly swept up. But his tenderness was as thorough in its destruction as any tornado.

His lips, full, firm yet somehow soft, brushed over hers. Pressed, then withdrew. Rubbed, cajoled, gave her enough of him, but waited until she granted him more. On the tail end of a sigh she couldn't contain, she parted for him. Welcomed the penetration of his tongue. Slid into a sensual dance with him. It was she who sucked him, licking the roof of his mouth, sampling the dark, heady flavor of his groan. She who first brought teeth into play, nipping at the corner of his mouth, raking them down his chin, only to return to take just as he'd invited her to do.

She who crawled onto his lap, jerking her skirt up and straddling his powerful thighs.

But it was he who threw oil onto their fire, ratcheting their desire from a blaze into a consuming inferno.

With a snarl that vibrated through his chest and over her nipples, he tugged her head back and opened his mouth over her neck. She arched into the hot, wet caress of tongue and teeth, her hands shifting from his shoulders to his hair and holding on. Every flick and suck echoed low in her belly, between her thighs. Fleetingly, the thought that she should be embarrassed at how drenched her panties were flitted through her head. But the clamp of his hand on her hip and the roll of his hips, stroking the hard, thick length of his cock over her sex, obliterated every rationalization.

Think? All she could do was *feel.*

Pleasure, its claws tipped with greed, tore at hcr. She whimpered, clung to him.

"Again," she ordered. Begged. Didn't matter. As long as he did it *again.*

"That's it," he praised against her throat, licking a path to her ear, where he nipped the outer curve. Hell, when had *that* become an erogenous zone? "Tell me what you want, what you need from me. I'll give it to you, sweetheart. You just have to ask."

Keep turning me inside out. Keep holding me like I'm wanted, cherished. Keep making me forget who I am.

But those pleas veered too close to exposing that part of her she'd learned to protect with the zeal of a dragon guarding a treasure.

So instead she gave him what she could. What she'd be too embarrassed to admit in the light of day. "Here." With trembling, jerky movements, she yanked down the top of her dress, drew him to her bared breasts. "Kiss me. Mark me."

He followed through on his promise, giving her what she'd requested. His tongue circled her nipple, lapped at it, swirled before sucking so hard the corresponding ache twinged deep and high inside her. She tried to hold in her cry but couldn't. Not when lust arrowed through her, striking at the heart of her. He murmured against her flesh, switching breasts, and treating her other peak to the same erotic torture. Skillful fingers plucked and pinched the tip that was damp from his mouth.

"More," she gasped. "Oh, God, more."

"Tell me." The hand on her hip tightened, and he delivered another slow, luxurious stroke to her empty, wet sex. "Tell me once more. I want your voice, your words."

Frustration, the last stubborn remnants of shyness and passion warred within her. Her lips moved, but the demand *make me come* that howled inside her head refused to emerge. Finally she grabbed the hand at her waist and slid it over her hiked-up dress, down her inner thigh and between her legs. She pressed his palm to her, moaning at the temporary relief of him cupping her.

"You're cheating," he teased, but the almost guttural tone had her hips bucking against him. As did his, "You're soaked. For me."

"Yes," she rasped. "For you. Only for you." Truth. That piece of herself, she offered him. She'd never been this hungry, this desperate before. Not even for—*no!*

She flung herself away from the intrusive thought. Not here. In this hall, there was only room for her and this nameless, faceless man, who nonetheless handled her like the most desirable, beautiful creature he'd ever held. Or at least that's what she was convincing herself of for these stolen moments.

"Touch me," she whispered, grinding down against his hand. "Please touch me."

The fingers still sweeping caresses over her nipple abandoned her flesh to cradle her face. He tipped her head down until their mouths met. "Don't beg me to touch you," he said, his lips grazing hers with each word. "You'll never have to beg me to do that."

He sealed the vow with a plunge of his finger inside her.

She cried out, tossing her head back on her shoulders as pleasure rocked through her like an earthquake, cracking her open, exposing her.

"Damn," he swore. "So damn tight. So damn…" He bit off the rest of his litany, slowly pulling free of her, then just as slowly, just as tenderly thrusting back inside. But she didn't want slow, didn't want tender. And she told him so with a hard, swift twist of her hips, taking him deeper. "Sweetheart," he growled, warned.

"No," she panted. "I need to… Please." He'd said she didn't need to plead with him, but if it would get her what she craved—release, oblivion—she wasn't above it.

With a snarl, he crushed his mouth to hers, tongue driving between her lips as he buried himself inside her. She moaned into his kiss, even as she spread her legs wider, granting him deeper access to her body. And he took it. He withdrew one finger and returned to her with two, working them into her flesh, working *her.*

Something snapped within her, and she rode his hand, rode the exquisite storm he whipped to a frenzy with every stroke, every brush of his thumb over her clit, every curl of his fingertips on that place high and deep in her sex. He played her, demanding her body sing for him. And God, did it.

With one last rub over that, before now, untouched place, she splintered, screaming into his mouth. And he swallowed it, clutching her to him, holding her tight as she crashed headlong into the abyss, a willing sacrifice to pleasure.

* * *

Isobel snuggled under her warm blanket, grabbing ahold of those last few moments of lazy sleepiness before Aiden cried out, demanding she come free him from his crib and feed him. She sighed, curling into her pillow…

Wait. Her pillow wasn't this firm. Frowning, she rolled over…or tried to roll over. Something prevented the movement…

Oh, hell.

Not something. Some*one*.

She stiffened as reality shoved the misty dredges of sleep away and dragged in all the memories of the night before. Gala. Blackout. Finding a mysterious man. Calming him. Laughing with him. Kissing him…

She jerked away, her lashes lifting.

Weak, hazy pink-and-orange light poured in through the large window at the end of the hall. Morning, but just barely. So maybe about six o'clock. Still, the dawn-tinged sky provided enough light to realize the warm blanket was really a suit jacket. Instead of a mattress, she perched on a strong pair of muscular thighs. And her pillow was a wide, solid chest covered in a snow-white dress shirt.

Heart pounding like a heavy metal-drum solo, she inched her gaze up to the patch of smooth golden skin exposed by the buttons undone at a powerful throat. Her belly clenched, knots twisting and pulling tight as she continued her wary, slow perusal.

A carved-from-a-slab-of-stone jaw dusted with dark stubble.

An equally hard chin with just the faintest hint of a cleft.

A beautiful, sensual mouth that promised all kinds of decadent, corrupting pleasures. Pleasures she had firsthand knowledge that he could deliver. She clearly remembered sinking her teeth into the bottom, slightly fuller curve.

Suppressing a shiver that he would surely feel, as they were pressed so closely together, she continued skimming her gaze upward past a regal, patrician nose and sharp, almost harsh cheekbones.

As she raised her scrutiny that last scant inch to his eyes, his dense, black, ridiculously long lashes lifted.

She sucked in a painful breath. And froze. Except for her frantic pulse, which reverberated in her head like crashing waves relentlessly striking the shore. Deafening her.

Not because of the striking, piercing amber eyes that could've belonged to a majestic eagle.

No. Because she recognized those eyes.

It'd been two years since they'd coldly stared at her over a yawning, freshly dug grave with a flower-strewn mahogany casket suspended above it. But she'd never forget them.

Darius King.

Gage's best friend.

The man who blamed her for Gage's death.

The man who hated her.

Hated her... Hated her... As the words—and the throbbing pain of them—sank into her brain, her paralysis shattered. She scrambled off him, uncaring of how clumsy her backward crab-walk appeared. She just needed to be away from him. From the shock that quickly bled from his gaze and blazed into rage and disgust.

God, no. How could she have kissed…touched… Let him…

You're fucking him, aren't you? Admit it, goddamn you. Admit it! You're fucking my best friend! You whore!

The memory of Gage's scream ricocheted off the walls of her skull, gaining volume and power by the second. Darius hadn't been the first man he'd thought she'd been cheating with—not even the third or fifth. But she'd never seen him as enraged, as out-of-control at the thought of her being with this man. Gage had never physically abused her during their marriage, but that night… That night she'd truly been afraid he would hit her.

Afterward she'd made a conscious effort to not look at Darius, not be alone in the same room with him if she couldn't avoid him altogether. Even after he'd married an iceberg of a woman, she'd maintained her distance.

And now, not only had she laughed and talked with him, but she had allowed him inside her body. She'd allowed him to bring her the most soul-shattering pleasure.

Meeting his stare, she could read the condemnation there. The confirmation that she was indeed the whore Gage had called her.

Humiliation, hurt and fury—at him and herself—barreled through her, propelling her to her feet. Snatching up her purse and shoes, she clutched them to her chest.

"Isobel." The voice that had caressed her ears with its deep, melodious tone, that had stirred desire with explicit words, now caused ice to coat her veins. Gage used to take great delight in telling her how much his friend disliked her. Though she now knew when her husband's lips were moving, he was lying, hearing Darius's frigid disdain directed at her, meeting his derisive gaze… She believed it now, just as she had then.

"I-I…" She dragged in a breath, shaking her head as she backpedaled. "I need to go. I'm sorry," she rasped.

Hating that she'd apologized, that she sounded scared and…broken, she whirled around and damn near sprinted down the thankfully empty hallway, not feeling the cold marble under her feet. Or the stone as she escaped the mansion. None of the valets from the night before appeared, but she'd glimpsed the direction in which they'd driven off and followed that path.

Twenty minutes later, with keys snatched from the valet stand and car successfully located, she exited onto the freeway. Though with every mile she steadily placed between her and the mansion—and Darius—she couldn't shake the feeling of being pursued.

Couldn't shake the sense that she could run, but couldn't hide.

But that damn sure wouldn't stop her from trying.

Three

Darius stood outside the weathered brick apartment building, the chill of the October morning not having evaporated yet.

At eight thirty, the overcast sky didn't add any cheer to this South Deering neighborhood. The four rows of identical windows facing the front sported different types of shades, and someone had set potted plants with fake flowers by the front entrance, but nothing could erase the air of poverty that clung to this poor, crime-stricken section of the city. Foam cups, paper and other bits of trash littered the patch of green on the left side of the apartment complex. Graffiti and gang tags desecrated the side of the neighboring building. It sickened him that only thirty minutes away, people lived in almost obscene wealth, a good many of them willingly choosing to pretend this kind of poverty didn't exist. He'd been born into those rarefied circles, but he wasn't blind to the problems of classism, prejudice and ignorance that Chicago faced.

Still… Gage's son was growing up here, in this place that hovered only steps above a tenement. And that ate at Darius like the most caustic acid.

Stalking up the sidewalk, he approached the front entrance. A lock sat above the handle, but on a whim, he tugged on it, and the door easily opened.

"You have to be kidding me," he growled. Anyone off the street could walk into the building, leaving all the residents here vulnerable where they should feel safest. Aiden being one of the most vulnerable.

Darius stepped into the dimly lit foyer, the door shutting behind him. Rectangular mailboxes mounted the wall to his right, and to his left, the steel doors to an elevator. In front of him, a flight of stairs stretched to the upper floors. With one last glance at the elevator doors, he headed for the stairs. He wasn't trusting the elevator in a building this damn old.

According to the information his investigator had provided, Isobel lived on the third floor. He climbed several flights of stairs and entered the door that led to her level. Like the lobby, the hallway was clean, even if the carpet was threadbare. Bulbs lit the area, and the paint, while not fresh, wasn't as desperately in need of a new coat as the downstairs. The broken lock on the front door notwithstanding, it appeared as if the landlord, or at least the residents, cared about their home.

Seconds later, he arrived in front of Isobel's apartment door, standing on a colorful welcome mat depicting a sleeping puppy. It should've seemed out of place, but oddly it didn't strike him that way. But it did serve to remind him that a young boy lived behind the closed door. A boy who deserved to live in a home where he and the puppy could run free and play. A place with a yard, a swing set.

A safe place.

Anger rekindled in his chest, and raising his fist, he knocked on the door. Moments passed, and it remained shut. He rapped on the door again. And still no one answered.

Suppressing a growl, he tucked his hands into the pockets of his coat and narrowed his gaze on the floor.

"Isobel, I know you're home. I can see the shadow of your feet. So open the door," he ordered.

Several more seconds passed before the sound of locks twisting and disengaging reached him, and then she stood in the entrance.

He deliberately inhaled a calming breath. For the entire drive from his Lake Forest home, he'd tried to prepare himself for seeing her again. It'd been a week since the night of the blackout. A week since he'd suffered a panic attack, and she'd held his hand and dragged him back from the edge with her teasing, silly conversation and lilting laughter. A week since he'd feasted on her mouth, experienced the tight-as-hell grip of her body spasming around his fingers, and her greedy cries of pleasure splintering around his ears.

A week since he woke and the piercing anticipation of finally glimpsing the face of the mysterious woman he'd embraced faded into a bright, hot anger as he realized her true identity.

Yes, he'd tried to ready himself for the moment they'd face each other again. And staring down at her now, with all that long, thick hair tumbling over her shoulders, framing a beautiful face with fey eyes that should have existed only within the pages of a fantasy novel, his attempt at preparation had been for shit. Even in a faded pink tank top and cotton pajama pants, with what appeared to be fat leprechauns and rainbows, she knocked him on his ass.

And he resented her for it. Hated himself more.

Because no matter how he tried, he couldn't forget how she'd burned in his arms that night. Exploded. Never had a woman been that uninhibited and hot for him. She'd scorched him so that even now—even a week later—he still felt the marks on his fingers, his chest, his cock. He had an inkling why his best friend had been driven crazy because of her infidelities.

Because imagining Isobel aflame like that with another man had a green-tinted anger churning his own gut.

Which was completely ridiculous. Gage had tortured himself over this woman. It would be a breezy spring day in hell before Darius allowed himself to be her next victim.

"What do you want?" Isobel asked, crossing her arms under her breasts. Her obviously braless breasts.

"To talk," he said, trying and failing to completely keep the snap out of his voice. "And I'd rather not do it out in the hallway."

Her delicate chin kicked up, and even though she stood almost a foot shorter than his own six feet three inches, she continued defiantly standing there, a female Napoleon guarding her empire. "We don't have anything to talk about, so whatever you came here to say should be a very short conversation. The hallway is as good a place as any."

"Fine." He smiled, and it must have appeared as false as it felt because her eyes narrowed on him. "But the private investigator I hired to find you also spoke with your neighbors. Including a Mrs. Gregory, who lives across the hall. A lovely woman, from what he tells me. Seventy-three, lives alone, never misses an episode of the *Young and the Restless* and is a terrible gossip. At this very moment, she probably has her ear against the door, trying to eavesdrop on our conversation. So if you don't mind her finding out where you spent the night of the blackout—and *how* you spent it—I don't either."

Her head remained tilted at that stubborn angle, and the flat line of her mouth didn't soften. But she did slant a glance around him to peek at the closed door across the hall. Whatever she saw made her lips flatten even more.

"Come in." She stepped back, allowing him to pass by her. When he moved into the tiny foyer, she called out, "Good morning, Mrs. Gregory," and shut the door. "I swear that woman could tell the cops where Jimmy Hoffa is buried," she muttered under her breath.

Humor, unexpected and unwelcome, rippled through his chest. He remembered this about her from the night of the blackout. Funny, self-deprecating, charming.

Given everything he knew of Isobel's character, the side she'd shown him in the darkness must've been a charade.

Her shock and horror the following morning had been real, though.

He gave his head a mental shake. He wasn't here to rehash the colossal mistake he'd committed in the dark. He had a purpose, an agenda. And before he left this morning, it would be accomplished.

Making resolve a clear, hard wall in his chest, he moved into the living room. Well, *moved* was generous. The change in location from foyer to the main room only required two steps.

Jesus, the whole apartment could fit into his great room—three times. The living room and dining room melded into one space, only broken up by a small counter that separated it from the equally small kitchen. A cramped tunnel of a hallway shot off to the left and led to what he knew from floorplans of the building to be a miniscule bedroom, bathroom and closet.

At least it was clean. The obviously secondhand couch, coffee table and round dining table wore signs of life—scratches, scuff marks and ragged edges in the upholstery. But everything was neat and shined, the scent of pine and lemon a pleasant fragrance under the aroma of brewing coffee. Even the colorful toys—blocks, a plastic easel, a colorful construction set and books—were stacked in chaotic order in one corner.

A hard tug wrenched his gut to the point of pain at the sight of those symbols of childhood. A tug that resonated with yearning. Aiden had been only six months old the last time Darius had seen him. That'd been at Gage's funeral. How much had the boy changed in the two years since? Had his light brown hair darkened to the nearly black of Gage's own color? As he'd matured, had he grown to resemble his mother, or had he inherited more of his father's features?

That had been the seed of Gage's and the family's doubts regarding the baby's parentage. The boy had possessed neither Gage's nor Isobel's features, except for her eyes. So they'd assumed he must look like his father—his true father. That Isobel had refused a paternity test had further solidified their suspicions that Gage hadn't been Aiden's father. And then, out of spite, she'd made Gage choose—his family or her. Of course, out of love and loyalty, and foolish blindness, he'd chosen her, isolating himself from his parents and friends. Till the end.

Selfish. Conniving. Cold.

Except maybe not so cold. Darius had a firsthand example of how hot she could burn…

Shit.

Focus.

Unbuttoning his jacket, he turned and watched Isobel stride toward him. She did another of those chin lifts as she entered the living room. Jesus, even with suspicion heavy in those blue-gray eyes, they were striking. Haunting. Beautiful.

Deceitful.

"You're not going to ask me to have a seat?" he drawled, the dark, twisted mix of bitterness and lust grinding relentlessly within him.

"Since you won't be staying long, no," she replied, crossing her arms over her chest again. "What do you want?"

"That's my question, Isobel." Without her invite, he lowered to the dark blue, worn armchair across from the couch. "What do you want? Why were you at the gala last week?"

"None of your business."

"See, that's where you're wrong. If you came there to pump the Wellses for money, then it is most definitely my business," he said. Studying her, he caught the flash of emotion in her eyes. Emotion, hell. Guilt. That flash had been guilt. Satisfaction, thick and bright, flared within him. "What happened, Isobel? Did whatever fool you sank your claws into out there in Los Angeles come to his senses and kick you out before you sucked him dry?"

She stared at him, slowly uncoiling her arms and sinking to a perch on her sofa. "The *poor fool* you're so concerned about was my Aunt Lila, who I stayed with to help her recover from a stroke," she continued, derision heavy in her voice. "She died a couple of months ago from another massive stroke, which is why I'm back here in Chicago. Any more insults or assumptions you want to throw out there before finally telling me why you're here?"

"I'm sorry for your loss," he murmured. And he was sorry. He, more than anyone, understood the pain of losing a loved one. But that's all he would apologize for. Protecting and defending his family from someone who sought to use them? No, he'd never regret that. "Now…

What do you want with the Wells family? Although—" he deliberately turned his head and scanned the tight quarters of her apartment, lingering on the pile of envelopes on the breakfast bar before returning his attention to her "—I can probably guess if you don't want to admit it."

Her shoulders rolled back, her spine stiffening. Even with her just-rolled-out-of-bed hair and clothes, she appeared…regal. Pride. It was the pride that clung to her as closely as the tank top molding to her breasts.

"What. Do. You. Want. With. Them?" he ground out, when she didn't answer.

"Help," she snapped, leaning forward, a matching anger lighting her arctic eyes. "I need their help. Not for me. I'd rather hang pictures and lay a welcome mat out in a freshly dug hole than go to them for anything. But for the grandson they've rejected and refused to acknowledge, I need them."

"You would have the nerve to ask them for help—no, let's call it what it is—for *money* and use your son to do it? The son you've kept from them for two years? That's low even for you, Isobel." The agony and helplessness over Gage's death, the rage toward the woman who was supposed to have loved him, but who had instead mercilessly and callously broken him, surged within him. Tearing through him like a sword, damn near slicing him in half. But he submerged the roiling emotions beneath a thick sheet of ice. "The answer is no. You don't get to decide when they can and can't have a relationship with the grandson who is the only part they have left of the son they loved and lost. You might be his *mother*, and I use that term loosely—"

"Get out." The quiet, sharp words cut him off. She stood, the fine tremor shivering through her body visible in the finger she pointed toward the door. "Get the hell out and don't come back."

"Not until we discuss—"

"You're just like them," she snarled, continuing as if he hadn't even spoken. "Cut from the same golden but filthy cloth. You don't know shit about me as a mother, because you haven't been there. You, Baron or Helena. So you have zero right to have an opinion on how I'm raising my son. And for the record, I didn't try to keep them from Aiden. They didn't want him. Didn't want to know him. Didn't even believe he was their grandson. So don't you dare walk in here, look at this apartment and judge me—"

"Oh, no, Isobel," he contradicted her, slowly rising to his feet as well, tired of her lies. Especially about the people, the *family*, who'd taken him in when he'd lost his own. Who'd accepted him as their own. "I judged you long before this. Your actions as a wife—" he spat the word out, distasteful on his tongue "—condemned you."

"Right." She nodded, a sneer matching his own, curling her mouth. "I was the money-grabbing, social-climbing whore who tricked Gage into marriage by getting knocked up. And he was the sacrificial lamb who cherished and adored me, who remained foolishly loyal to me right up until the moment of his death."

"Don't," he growled, the warning low, rough. He'd never called her a whore; he detested that word. Even when he'd discovered his ex-wife was fucking one of his vice presidents, Darius had never thrown that ugly name at her. Yet to hear Isobel talk about Gage in that dismissive manner when his biggest sin had been loving her… "You don't get to talk about him like that."

"Yes." Her harsh crack of laughter echoed in the room. "That's right, another rule I forgot from my time in my loving marriage. I don't get to speak until I'm spoken to. And even then, keep it short before I embarrass him and myself. Well, sorry to break it to you, but this isn't your home. It's mine, and I want you out—"

"Mommy." The small, childish voice dropped in the room like a hand grenade, cutting Isobel off. Both of them turned toward it. A toddler with dark, nearly black curls and round cheeks, and clad in Hulk pajamas, hovered in the entrance to the living room. Shuffling back and forth on his bare feet, he stuck his thumb into his mouth and glanced from Isobel to Darius before returning his attention to her.

Aiden.

An invisible fist bearing brass knuckles landed a haymaker against Darius's chest. The air in his lungs ejected on a hard, almost painful *whoosh*. He couldn't breathe, couldn't move. Not when his best friend's son dashed across the floor and threw his tiny but sturdy body at his mother, the action full of confidence that she would catch him. Which she did. Kneeling, Isobel gathered him in her arms, standing up and holding him close.

Over his mother's shoulder, Aiden stared at Darius with a gaze identical to Isobel's. A hand roughly the size of a toddler's reached into his chest and squeezed Darius's heart. Hard.

Christ.

He'd expected to be happy or satisfied at finally seeing Aiden. But he hadn't been prepared for this… this overwhelming joy or fierce protectiveness that swamped him, weakened his knees. Gage's son—and there was no mistaking he was indeed Gage's son. He might have Isobel's eyes, but the hair, the shape of his face, his brow, nose, the wide, smiling mouth… They were all his best friend.

The need to protect the boy intensified, swelled. Darius would do anything in his power to provide for him… raise him the way Gage didn't have the opportunity to do. Resolve shifting and solidifying in his chest, his paralysis broke, and he moved across the room, toward mother and son.

"Hello," he greeted Aiden, the gravel-roughened tone evidence of the emotional storm still whirling inside him.

Aiden grinned, and the tightening around Darius's ribcage increased.

"Aiden, this is Mr. King. Can you tell him hi?" Isobel shifted so she and Aiden faced Darius. Her voice might've been light and cheerful, but her eyes revealed that none of the anger from their interrupted conversation had abated. "Tell Mr. King, hi, baby," she encouraged.

"Hi, Mr. King," he mimicked. Though it actually sounded more like, *Hi, Mih Key.*

"Hi, Aiden," he returned, smiling. And unable to

help himself, he rubbed the back of a finger down the boy's warm, chubby cheek.

A soft catch of breath reluctantly tugged his attention away from the child. He glanced at Isobel, and she stared at him, barely blinking. After a moment, she shook her head, turning her focus back to her son.

What had that been about? He studied her, trying to decipher the enigma that was Isobel Hughes.

There's no enigma, no big mystery. Only what she allows you to see.

As the reminder boomed in his head, he frowned. His ex-wife had been an expert at hiding her true self until she'd wanted him to glimpse it. And that had only happened toward the end of the relationship, when both of them had stopped pretending they shared anything resembling a marriage. Not with her screwing other men, and Darius refusing to play the fool or pay for the black American Express card any longer.

"Want milk," Aiden demanded as Isobel settled him on the floor again. "And 'nana."

She brushed a hand over his curls, but the hair just fell back into his face. "You want cereal with your milk and banana?" she asked. Aiden nodded, smiling, as if congratulating her for understanding him. "Okay, but can you go play in the room while I fix it?"

Aiden nodded again, agreeing. "Go play."

She took his hand in hers and led him back down the hall, talking to him the entire time until they disappeared. Several minutes later, she returned alone, the adoring, gentle expression she gave her son gone.

"I have things to do, so..." She waved toward the

front door, but Darius didn't move. "Seriously, this is ridiculous," she snapped.

"He's Gage's son," he murmured.

Fire flared in her eyes as they narrowed. "Are you sure? You can tell that from just a glance at him? After all, I've been with so many men. Any of them could be his real father."

"Don't play the victim, Isobel. It doesn't fit," he snapped. "And I'm not leaving until we talk."

"I repeat," she ground out. "We have nothing to—"

"We're getting married."

She rocked back on her bare heels as if struck. Shock rounded her fairy eyes, parted her lips. She gaped at him, her fingers fluttering to circle her neck. He should feel regret at so bluntly announcing his intentions. Should. But he didn't.

He'd had a week to consider this idea. Yes, it seemed crazy, over-the-top, and he'd rejected it as soon as the thought had popped into his head. But it'd nagged at him, and the reasons why it would work eventually outweighed the ones why it wouldn't. Of all the words used to describe him, *impetuous* or *rash* weren't among them. He valued discipline and control, in business and in his personal life. His past had taught him both were important. It'd been an impromptu decision that had robbed him of both his parents, and an impulsive one that had led him to marry a woman he'd known for a matter of months. The same mistake Gage had made.

But this...proposition was neither. He'd carefully measured it, and though just the thought of tying himself to another manipulative woman sickened him, he was willing to make the sacrifice.

Whatever doubts might've lingered upon walking up to her building, they had disintegrated as soon as he'd laid eyes on Aiden.

"You're crazy," she finally breathed.

He smiled, and the tug to the corner of his mouth felt cynical, hard. "No. Just realistic." He slid his hands into the front pockets of his pants, cocking his head and studying her pale, damnably lovely features. "Regardless of what you believe, I'm not judging you on the neighborhood you live in or your home. But the fact is you aren't in the safest area of Chicago, and this building isn't a shining example of security. The lock on the front door doesn't work. Anyone could walk in here. The locks on your apartment door are for shit. There isn't an alarm system. What if someone followed you home and busted in here? You would have no protection—you or Aiden."

"So I have a security system installed and call the landlord about the locks on the building entrance and my door. Easy fixes, and none of them require marriage to a man I barely know who despises me."

"If they were easy fixes," he said, choosing to ignore her comment about his feelings toward her, "why haven't you done them?" He paused, because something flickered in her gaze, and a surge of both anger and satisfaction glimmered in his chest. "You have contacted your landlord," he stated, taking her silence as confirmation. "And he hasn't done a damn thing about it." He stepped forward, shrinking the space between them. "Pride, Isobel. You're going to let pride prevent you from protecting your son."

Lightning flashed in her gaze, and for a moment he found himself mesmerized by the display. Like a bolt of electricity across a morning sky.

"Let me enlighten you. Pride became a commodity I couldn't afford a long time ago. But in the last two years, I've managed to scrape mine back together again. And neither you nor the Wellses can have it. I'm not afraid to ask for help. That's why I was at the gala. Why I was willing to approach Baron and Helena again. *For my son*. But you're not here to offer me help. You're demanding I sell my soul to another devil, just with a different face and name. Well, sorry. I'm not going to play your game. Not when it won't only be me losing this time, but Aiden, as well."

"Selling your soul to the devil? Not playing the game?" he drawled. "Come now, Isobel. A poor college student nabbing herself the heir to a fortune? Trapping him with a pregnancy, then isolating him from his family? Cry me a river, sweetheart. I was there, so don't try to revise history to suit your narrative."

"You're just like him," she whispered.

Darius stifled a flinch. Then cursed himself for recoiling in the first place. Gage had been a good man—good to her.

"You have two choices," he stated. "One, agree to marry me and we both raise Aiden. Or two, disagree, and I'll place the full weight of my name and finances behind Baron and Helena to help them gain custody of Aiden."

She gasped and wavered on her feet. On instinct, he shifted forward, lifting his arms to steady her. But she backpedaled away from him, pressing a hand against the wall and holding up the other in a gesture that screamed *stop right there*.

"You," she rasped, shaking her head. "You wouldn't do that."

"I would," he assured her. "And I will."

"Why?" She straightened, lowering both arms, but the shadows darkening her eyes gathered. "Why would you do that? Why would they? Baron and Helena…they don't even believe Aiden is Gage's. They've wanted nothing to do with him since he was born. Why would they seek custody now?"

"Because he *is* their grandson. I'll convince them of that. And he deserves to know them, love them. Deserves to learn about his father and come to know him through his parents. Aiden is all Baron and Helena have left of Gage. And you would deprive them of that relationship. I won't let you." The unfairness of Isobel's actions, of her selfishness, gnawed at him. She hadn't witnessed the devastation Gage's death had left behind, the wreckage. Baron had suffered a heart attack not long after, and yes, most of it could be attributed to lifestyle choices. But the loss of his only son, that had definitely been a contributing factor.

Yet if they'd had Aiden in their lives during these last two difficult years…he could've been a joy to them. But Isobel had skipped town, not even granting them the opportunity to bond. If she'd stayed long enough, Baron and Helena would've done just what Darius had—taken one look at the child and *known* he belonged to Gage.

"And I won't let you make Aiden a pawn. Or worse, a substitute for Gage. *He won't become Gage*. I refuse to allow you and the Wellses to turn him into his father. I'll fight that with every breath in my body."

"He would be lucky to become like the man his father was," Darius growled. "To be loved by his parents. They welcomed me into their home, raised me when I had no one."

She didn't get to smear the family that had become his own. Gage had been his best friend, his confidante, his brother. Helena had stepped in as his mother. And Baron had been his friend, his mentor, his guiding hand in the multimillion-dollar financial-investment company Darius's father had left behind for his young, inexperienced son.

So no, she didn't get to malign them.

"I'm his mother," she said.

As if that settled everything.

When it didn't.

"And they're his grandparents," he countered. "Grandparents who can afford to provide a stable, safe, secure and loving home for him to thrive and grow in. He'll never want for anything, will have the best education and opportunities. Aiden should have all of his family in his life. You, me, his grandparents and aunt. He should enjoy a fulfilled, happy childhood, with the security of two parents and without the weight of struggle. With you marrying me, he will."

And the Wellses would avoid a prolonged custody

battle that could further tax Baron's health and possibly endanger his life. His recovery from the heart attack was going well, but Darius refused to add stress if he could avoid it.

Besides, as CEO and president of King Industries Unlimited, the conglomerate he'd inherited from his father, not only would Aiden be taken care of, but so would Isobel. She would want for nothing, have all the money available to satisfy her every materialistic need. He had experience with bearing the albatross of a greedy woman with Faith, his ex-wife, and though it galled him to have to repeat history, he'd rather take the financial hit than allow Isobel to extort more money from the Wellses. They'd protected him once, and he would gladly, willingly do the same for them.

"No." Isobel stared up at him, shoulders drawn back, hands curled into fists at her side. Though she still wore the evidence of her worry, she faced him like one general standing off against another. A glimmer of admiration slipped through his steely resolve. She'd reminded him of Napoleon earlier, and she did so again. But like that emperor, she would fail and eventually surrender. "I don't care how pretty you wrap it up, blackmail is still blackmail. And I'm not giving in to it. Now, for the last time, get out of my house."

"Call it what you want to help you sleep at night," he murmured. He reached inside his suit jacket and removed a silver business card holder. He withdrew one as he strode to the breakfast bar, and then set it on the counter. "Think carefully before you make a rash decision you'll regret. Here's where you can reach me."

She didn't reply, just stalked to the front door and yanked it open.

"This isn't anywhere near over, Isobel," he warned, exiting her apartment.

"Maybe it isn't for you. But for me, I'm going to forget all about you as soon as you get out." And with that parting shot, she closed the door shut behind him. Or more accurately, in his face.

He didn't immediately head down the hallway, instead pausing a moment to stare at the door. And smile.

He'd meant what he'd told her. This wasn't over.

And damn if he wasn't looking forward to the next skirmish.

Four

A week later, Isobel drove through the winding, tidy streets of Lake Forest. During the hour and fifteen minutes' drive from South Deering, the inner-city landscape gave way to the steel-and-glass metropolis of downtown, to the affluent suburb that made a person believe she'd stepped into a pretty New England town. The quaint ice cream shop, bookstore, gift shop and boutiques in the center of the town emanated charm and wealth. All of it practically shouted history, affluence and *keep the hell out, riffraff!*

She would be the aforementioned riffraff. Discomfort crawled down her neck. Her decade-old Honda Civic stuck out like a sore thumb among the Aston Martins, Bugattis and Mercedes Benzes like a poor American relation among its luxurious, foreign cousins. Her GPS announced her upcoming turn, and she returned her focus to locating Darius's home.

Minutes later, Siri informed her that she'd reached her destination.

Good. God.

She didn't know much about architecture other than what she retained from the shows on HGTV, but even she recognized the style of the three-story home as Georgian. Beautiful golden bricks—not the weathered, dull color of her own apartment building—formed the outside of the huge structure, with its sloped roof and attached garage. It curved in an arc, claiming the land not already seized by the towering maple trees surrounding the property. Black shutters framed the many windows that faced the front and bracketed the wide wine-red door.

"You are not in South Deering anymore," she murmured to herself.

No wonder Darius had scrutinized her tiny apartment with a slight curl to his lips. He called this beautiful, imposing mansion home. Her place must've appeared like a Hobbit hole to him. A Hobbit hole from the wrong side of the Shire tracks.

Sighing, she dragged her attention back to the reason she'd driven out here.

She had a marriage bargain to seal.

After climbing the three shallow steps that led to the front door, she rang the bell. Only seconds passed before it opened and—instead of a housekeeper or butler—Darius stood in the entryway.

It wasn't fair.

His masculine beauty. His affect on her.

She was well versed in the danger of handsome men. They used their appearance as a lure—a bright, sensual lure that entranced a woman, distracted her from the darkness behind the shiny exterior. And by the time a woman noticed, it was way too late…

Even though she was aware of the threat he presented, she still stared at him, fighting the carnal thrall he exuded like a pheromone. His dark brown hair waved away from his strong brow, emphasizing the slashing cheekbones, patrician nose, full lips and rock-hard jaw with the faint dent in the chin. And his eyes…vivid, golden and piercing. They unleashed a warm slide of heat in her veins, even as she fought the urge to duck her head and avoid that scalpel-sharp gaze.

With a quick glance, she took in the black turtleneck and slacks that draped over his powerful shoulders, wide chest and muscular thighs. It didn't require much effort to once again feel those thighs under hers or recall the solid strength of his chest under her hands. Her body tingled with the memory, as if he'd imprinted himself in her skin, in her senses, that night. And no matter how she tried, she couldn't evict him.

"Isobel." The way that low, cultured drawl wrapped around her name was indecent. "Come in."

She dipped her chin in acknowledgment and moved forward. Doing her best not to touch him, she still couldn't avoid breathing in his delicious scent—cedar and sun-warmed air, with a hint of musk that was all male. All him. She'd tried her best to forget the flavor of him from that night, too. Epic fail.

The heels of her boots clacked against the hardwood floor of the foyer, and she almost bent to remove them, not wanting to make scuff marks. She studied the house, not even attempting to hide her curiosity. Yes, the inside lived up to the splendor of the exterior. A wide staircase swept to an upper level, and two airy rooms extended from each side of the entryway. Huge fireplaces, furniture that belonged in magazines and rugs that could've taken up space in museums. And windows. So many windows, which offered views of acres of land.

But she examined her surroundings for hints into the man who owned the home. Framed photos lined the mantel in one of the living rooms, but she couldn't glimpse the images from this distance. Were they of the parents he'd told her about during the blackout? Were they of Gage, when they were teens? Around the time he'd saved Darius's life? Did the photographs contain images of the Wellses?

Her survey swept over the expected but beautiful portraits of landscapes and zeroed in on a glass-and-weathered-wood box. A step closer revealed a collection of antique pocket watches. She shifted her inspection to Darius, who watched her, his expression shuttered. Oh, there had to be a story there.

But she wasn't here to find it out.

"You know why I'm here," she said. "I'd like to get this over with."

"We can talk in the study." He turned, and after a moment of hesitation, she followed.

They entered the massive room, where two walls were floor-to-ceiling windows and the other two were filled with books. A large, glossy black desk dominated one end, and couches, armchairs and an immense fireplace claimed the rest. It invited a person to grab a book and settle in for a long read. She couldn't say how she knew, but she'd bet her last chocolate bar that Darius spent most of his time here.

"So, you've come to a decision." He perched on the edge of his desk and waved toward one of the armchairs. "Please, have a seat."

"No, thank you," Isobel murmured. "I—" She swallowed, for an instant unable to force the words past her suddenly constricted throat. A wave of doubt assailed her, but she broke through it. This was the right decision. "I'll agree to marry you."

She expected a gloating smile or a smirk. Something that boasted, *I win.*

Instead his amber gaze studied her, unwavering and intense. Once more she had the inane impression that he could see past her carefully guarded shields to the vulnerable, confused and scared woman beneath. Her head argued it was impossible, but her heart pounded in warning. His figuring out her fears and insecurities when it came to the situation and *him* would be disastrous.

"What made you change your mind?" he asked.

No way was she telling him about arriving home with Aiden after work one night last week to find the police staked out in front of her building because of a burglary and assault. It'd only nailed home Darius's warning about the unsafety of her environment—for her and for Aiden.

Instead she shrugged. "Does it matter?"

"This was a hard decision for you, wasn't it?" he murmured.

Anger flared inside her like a struck match. "Why would you say that? Maybe I just held out longer so you wouldn't guess how giddy I am to have a chance at all your money? Or maybe I was hoping you would just offer more. I'm a mercenary, after all, always searching for the next opportunity to fill my pockets." His mouth hardened into a firm line, but she didn't care. She was only stating what they both knew he thought of her character. Straightening from the chair, she crossed her arms over her chest and hiked her chin up. "Like I said, I'll agree to marry you, but I have a few conditions first. And they're deal breakers."

He nodded, but the slight narrowing of his eyes relayed his irritation. Over her sarcasm or her stipulations, she couldn't tell, but in the end, neither mattered. Just as long as he conceded.

"First, you must promise to place Aiden, his welfare and protection above anything else. Including the Wellses' needs and agenda."

Another nod, but this one was tighter. And the curves of his mouth remained flattened, grim. As if he forced himself to contain words he wanted to say. If that were the case, he controlled it, and she continued.

"Second, I'm Aiden's mother, and since he's never known a father, you'll fill that role for him. If you don't, I won't go through with this. If you can't love and accept him as if he's your own blood, your son, then we're done. I won't have him hurt or rejected. Or worse, feel like he doesn't belong." Like she had. The soul-deep pain of being unworthy had wounded her, and she still bore the scars. She wouldn't subject Aiden to that kind of hurt. Even if it meant going to court.

"He *is* my blood," Darius said, and she blinked, momentarily stunned by his fierceness. "Gage and I might not have shared the same parents, but in all other ways we were brothers. And his son will be mine, and I'll love Aiden how his father would have if he'd lived and had the chance."

Satisfaction rolled in, flooding her and sweeping away the last of her doubts surrounding that worry. Even if Darius knew next to nothing about the man he called his brother. She believed him when he said he'd love Aiden how Gage *should have*.

"Which brings me to my next concern. I'm Aiden's mother and have been making all decisions regarding him since he was born. I'm not going to lie and claim including you will be an easy adjustment, but I promise to try. But that said, we're his parents, and we will make those decisions together. Us. Without interference from the Wellses."

"Isobel," he growled, pushing off the desk. He stalked a step closer to her, but then drew to an abrupt halt. Shoving a hand through his hair, he turned his head to stare out the window, a tic pulsing along his clenched jaw.

Cursing herself for doing it, she regarded the rigid line. That night when they'd been two nameless, faceless people in the dark, she hadn't needed sight to tell how strong and hard his jaw had been. Her fingers and lips had relayed the information.

God, she needed to stop dwelling on that night. It was gone, and for all intents and purposes, it didn't happen. It'd disappeared as soon as the morning light had dawned.

"Isobel." He returned his attention to her, and she braced herself for both the impact of his gaze and his words. "I agree with your conditions, but they are his grandparents. And you need to understand that I won't keep him away from them."

Like you have. The accusation remained unsaid, but it screamed silently in the room.

"I emailed Baron and Helena pictures of Aiden after I left for California. And when every one of those messages bounced back as if I'd been blocked, I mailed them, along with letters telling them how he was doing and growing. But they came back unopened, marked 'return to sender.' So I didn't keep him from them. They kept themselves out of his life."

Darius frowned. "Why would they lie about that?"

"Yes. Why would they lie about that?" She shook her head, holding up a hand when his lips parted to what would, no doubt, be another defense of his friend's family. "I have one last condition."

She paused, this one more difficult than the previous ones. Demanding things on Aiden's behalf proved easy for her. But this one… This one involved her and Darius. And it acknowledged that something had happened between them. That "something" being he'd made her body sing like an opera diva hitting notes high enough to shatter glass.

"What is it?" Darius asked when she didn't immediately state the added rule.

"No sex," she blurted out. Mentally rolling her eyes at herself, she inhaled a deep breath and tried it again. "This arrangement is in name only. No sex."

He stilled, his powerful body going motionless. Shadows gathered in his gaze, broiling like a storm building on a dark horizon.

"I guess I need to applaud your honesty," he drawled. "This time around, you're being up front about your plans to betray your husband with another man."

Fury scalded her, and as unwise as it was, she stalked forward, until only inches separated them. "You're so damn sure of yourself. It must be nice to know everything and have all the answers. To be so sure you have all the facts, when in truth you don't. Know. A. Damn. Thing," she bit out.

He lowered his head until their noses nearly bumped, and his breath coasted across her mouth. She could taste his kiss, the sinful, addictive flavor of it.

Memories bombarded her. Memories of his lips owning hers, taking, giving. Of his hands cupping her breasts, tweaking the tips that even now ached and taunted beneath her bra. Of his fingers burying themselves inside her over and over, stroking places inside her that had never been touched before.

Of his cock, so hard and demanding beneath her…

"So you don't care if I take another woman?" he pressed, shifting so another inch disappeared.

An image of him covering someone else, moving over her, straining against her…driving into her, filled her head. A hot wave of anger swamped her, green-tipped claws raking her chest. Her fingers curled into her palms, but she shook her head. Whether it was to rid herself of the mental pictures or in denial of the emotion that smacked of jealousy—a jealousy she had no business, no right, to feel—she didn't know.

"No," she lied, retreating. "Just respect my son and me."

The corner of his mouth tipped into a scornful half smile. "Of course," he said, the words containing more than a hint of a sneer. "Now I have a couple of conditions. The first, we marry in three months. That should give you plenty of time to become accustomed to the arrangement, me and condition number two. You and Aiden are going to move in with me."

Oh, hell no. "No, not happening."

He nodded. "Yes, you are," he contradicted, the flint in his voice echoed in his eyes. "That's my deal breaker. One of my reasons for this whole arrangement is for Aiden to be raised in a safe, secure environment. He'll have both here."

"Okay, fine. I understand that. But why do we need to live with you. We could find an apartment or home in Edison Park or Beverly—"

"No," he stated flatly, cutting her protest off at the knees. "You'll both live here, and Aiden will know a home with two parents. This isn't a point for discussion, Isobel."

Shit. Living under the same roof as Darius? That

would be like Eve sleeping under the damn apple tree. Temptation. Trouble. But what option did she have? Sighing, she pinched the bridge of her nose. Okay, she could do it. Besides, this house was huge. She didn't even have to occupy the same side as Darius.

"Fine," she breathed. "Is there anything else?" She had the sudden need to get out of the house. Away from him. At least until she had no choice but to share his space.

"One last thing," he said, his tone deepening, sending an ominous tremor skipping up her spine. "Say my name."

She stared at him, not comprehending his request. No, his order.

"What?"

"Say my name, Isobel," he repeated.

Tilting her head to the side, she conceded warily. "Darius."

Heat flashed in his eyes, there and gone so fast, she questioned whether she imagined it. "That's the first time you've said my name since that morning."

He didn't need to specify to which morning he referred. But the first time… That couldn't be true. They'd had several conversations, or confrontations, since then… Then again, if it were true…

"Why does it matter?" she asked, something dark, complicated and hot twisting her stomach, pooling lower. "Why do you want to hear me say your name?"

He stared at her, the silence growing and pulsing until its deafening heartbeat filled the room. Her own heart thudded against her sternum, adding to the rhythm.

"Because I've wanted to know what it sounds like on your tongue," he said, his voice quiet.

But so loud it rang in her ears. *On your tongue.* The words, so charged with a velvet, sensual promise, or threat—she couldn't decide which—ricocheted against the walls of her head.

She shivered before she could check her telltale reaction. And those eagle eyes didn't miss it. They turned molten, and his nostrils flared, his lips somehow appearing fuller, more carnal.

Danger.

Every survival instinct she possessed blared the warning in bright, blinking red. And in spite of the warmth between her legs transforming to an aching pulse, she heeded it.

Without a goodbye, she whirled around and got the hell out of there.

Maybe one day she could discover the trick to outrunning herself.

But for now, escaping Darius would have to do.

Five

Darius passed through the iron gate surrounding the Wellses' Gold Coast mansion and climbed the steps to the front door. The limestone masterpiece had been in their family for 120 years, harkening back to a time when more than the small immediate family lived under its sloped-and-turreted slate roof. As he twisted his key in the lock and pushed the heavy front door open, he considered himself blessed to be counted among that family. Not by blood, but by choice and love.

After entering the home, he bypassed the formal living and dining areas, and moved toward the rear of the home, the multihued glow from the stained-glass skylight guiding his way. This time of day, a little after five o'clock, Baron should have arrived home from the office. Since his heart attack, he'd cut his work days shorter. Helena and Gabriella should also be home, since they served dinner at six o'clock sharp every evening. In the chaotic turns Darius's life had suffered, this routine and the surety of family tradition had been—and still was—a reassurance, one strong, steady stone in a battered foundation.

But tonight, with the news he had to deliver, he hated potentially being the one taking a hammer to them.

"Darius," Helena greeted, rising from the feminine couch that had been her domain as long as he could remember. The other members of the family could occupy the armchairs or the other sofa, but the small, antique couch was all hers, like a queen with her throne. "There you are."

She crossed the room, clasping his hands in hers and rising on her toes. Obediently, he lowered his head so she could press her lips to one cheek and then the other. Her floral perfume drifted to his nose and wrapped him in the familiarity of home. "I have to admit we've all been discussing you, wondering what it is you have to talk to us about. You're being so mysterious."

She smiled at him, and her expression only increased the unease sitting in his gut. He'd called to give them a heads-up without relaying the reason. This kind of information—about his impending marriage—required a face-to-face conversation.

"Hi, son." Baron came forward and patted him on the shoulder, enfolding Darius's hand in his. Warmth swirled in his chest, as it did every time the man he admired claimed him. "Sit and please tell us your news. Helena and Gabriella have been driving me crazy with their guessing. Do us all a favor and put them out of their gossipy misery."

"Oh, it's just been us, hmm?" Gabriella teased, arching an eyebrow at her father. She turned to Darius and handed him a glass of the Remy Martin cognac he preferred. "He wasn't exactly tuning out over the gossip about the blackout. It seems several people have leveled suits against Richard Dent, the tech billionaire who owns the mansion, for emotional distress. Apparently his apology for trapping people in overnight wasn't enough." She shook her head. "I didn't see him, but I even hear Gideon Knight was there. Can you imagine being caught in the dark with *him*?"

"I've met the man," Darius said, referring to the financial genius who'd launched a wildly successful start-up a couple of years ago. "He's reserved, but not as formidable as people claim."

He accepted the drink, bending to brush a kiss across Gabriella's cheek. She clasped his other hand in hers, squeezing it before releasing him to sit on a chair adjacent to her mother. He sank onto one across from her, while, with a sigh, Baron lowered to the largest armchair in the small circle.

Darius shot him a glance. "How're you feeling, Baron?"

"Fine, fine." He waved off the concerned question. "I'm just old," he grumbled.

After studying him for another few seconds, Darius finally nodded, but his worry over causing Baron more stress with his announcement doubled. Even so, he had to tell them, rather than have them discover the truth from another source.

"You already know Isobel Hughes has returned to Chicago."

All warmth disappeared from Helena's face, her gaze freezing into emerald chips of ice, her lips thinning. Gabriella wore a similar expression, but Baron's differed from the women in his family. Instead of furious, he appeared…tired.

"Yes," Helena hissed. "Gabriella told us Isobel showed up at the gala. How dare she?" she continued. "I would've had her arrested immediately."

"Attending a social event isn't a punishable offense, honey," Baron said, his tone weary.

His wife aimed a narrow-eyed glare in his direction, while Gabriella shook her head. "She's lucky the blackout occurred. Criminal or not, I would've had her escorted from the premises."

Leaning forward and propping his elbows on his spread knees, Darius sighed. "I have an announcement, and it concerns Isobel…and her son. I've asked her to marry me, and I'll become Aiden's stepfather."

A heavy silence plummeted into the room. They gaped at him, or at least Helena and Gabriella did. Again, Baron's reaction didn't coincide with his wife's or daughter's. He didn't glare at Darius, just studied him with a measured contemplation, his fingers templed beneath his chin.

"Are you insane?" Gabriella rasped. She jolted from the chair as if propelled from a cannon. Fury snapped in her eyes. But underneath, Darius caught the shivering note of hurt and betrayal. "Darius, what are you thinking?"

"You saw for yourself what she did to Gage, how she destroyed him. How could you even contemplate tying yourself to that woman?" Helena demanded, her voice trembling.

Pain radiated from his chest, pulsing and hot, with the knowledge that he was hurting the two women he loved most in the world. "I—"

"He's doing it for us," Baron declared, his low baritone quieting Helena's and Gabriella's agonized tirades. "He's marrying her so we can have a relationship with the boy."

"Is this true?" Helena demanded. Darius nodded, and she spread her bejeweled hands wide, shaking her head. "But why? He's not even our grandson."

"He is," Darius stated, his tone brooking no argument. "I've seen him," he added, softening his tone. "He's definitely Gage's son."

Gabriella snorted, crossing her arms over her chest. "You'll forgive us if we don't trust her lying, cheating words."

"Then trust mine."

He and Gabriella engaged in a visual standoff for several seconds before she spun on her heel and stalked across the room, toward the small bar.

"Gabriella's right," Helena said. "Sentimentality could be coloring your opinion, have you seeing a resemblance to Gage because you want there to be one." She paused, her pale fingers fluttering to her throat. "That she refused to have a DNA test done after his birth solidified that he wasn't Gage's son, for me. If he was, she wouldn't have been afraid to have one performed. No." She shook her head. "She's caused too much harm to this family," Helena continued. "I can't forget how she isolated Gage from us, so he had to sneak away just to see us. She destroyed him. I'll never forgive her. Ever."

"And no one asked you to be our sacrificial lamb," Gabriella interjected. "What about your life, marrying someone you love?" she rasped. Clearing her throat, she crossed the room and handed her mother a glass of wine before returning to the chair she'd vacated. "There's a very reasonable solution, and it doesn't require you shackling yourself to a woman who's proven she can't be trusted. If by some miracle the child is really Gage's, then we can fight for custody. We would probably be more fit guardians than *her* anyway."

"Take a small boy away from the only parent he's ever known? Regardless of our opinion concerning her moral values, I've seen her with him. She adores him, and she's his world. It would devastate Aiden to be removed from her." And it would kill Isobel. Of that, Darius had zero doubt. "Isobel wouldn't give up custody without a hard battle, which would be taxing on all of you, too. No, this is the best solution for everyone." He met each of their eyes. "And it's done."

Several minutes passed, and Darius didn't try to fill the silence, allowing them the time to accept what he understood was hard news. But they didn't have a choice. None of them did.

"Thank you, Darius," Baron murmured. "I know this wasn't an easy decision, and we appreciate it, support you in it. Bringing the boy into his family—it's what Gage would've wanted. And we will respect Isobel as his mother...and your wife."

Helena emitted a strangled sound, but she didn't contradict her husband. Gabriella didn't either. But she stood once more and rushed from the room.

"Just be careful, Darius. I've lost one son to Isobel Hughes. I don't think I could bear it if I lost another," Helena pleaded, the pain in her softly spoken words like jagged spikes stabbing his heart. Rising, she cradled his cheek before following Gabriella.

"They'll be fine, son," Baron assured him.

Darius nodded, but apprehension settled in his chest, an albatross he couldn't shake off. His intentions were to unite this family, return some of Helena and Baron's joy by reconciling them with their son's child.

But staring at the entrance where Helena and Gabriella had disappeared, he prayed all his efforts wouldn't end up destroying what he desired to build.

Six

Isobel leaned over Aiden, gently sweeping her hand down his dark curls. After the excitement of moving into a new home and new room jammed with new toys and a race car bed he adored, Aiden had finally exhausted himself. She'd managed to get him fed, bathed and settled in for the night, and all while avoiding Darius.

It'd been a week since she'd agreed to the devil's bargain, and now, fully ensconced in his house, she could no longer use Aiden as an excuse to hide away. With a sigh, she ensured the night-light was on and exited the bedroom, leaving the door cracked behind her. She quietly descended the staircase and headed toward the back of the home, where the kitchen was. She would've preferred not to come downstairs at all, but her stomach rumbled.

The room followed what appeared to be the theme of the home—huge, with windows. Top-of-the-line appliances gleamed under the bright light of a crystal chandelier, and a butcher block and marble island dominated the middle of the vast space. A breakfast nook with a round table and four chairs added a sense of warmth and intimacy to the room. Isobel shook her head as she approached one of the two double-door refrigerators.

She should be grateful. But even now, standing in a kitchen her mother would surrender one of her beloved children to have, she couldn't escape the phantom noose slowly tugging tighter, strangling her. Powerlessness. Purposelessness. Futile anger. The emotions eddied and churned within her like a storm-tossed sea, pitching her, drowning her.

She'd promised herself two years ago that she'd never be at the mercy of another man. Yet if she didn't find some way to protect herself, maintain the identity of the woman she'd come to be, she would end up in a prison worthy of *Architectural Digest*.

Minutes later, she had the makings of a ham-and-cheese sandwich on the island. Real ham—none of that convenience-store deli ham for Darius King—and some kind of gourmet cheese that she could barely pronounce but that tasted like heaven.

"Isobel."

She glanced up from layering lettuce and tomatoes onto her bread to find Darius in the entrance. Her fingers froze, as did the rest of her body. Would this deep, acute awareness occur every time she saw him?

It zipped through her body like an electrical current, lighting every nerve ending.

"Darius," she replied, bowing her head back over her dinner.

Though she'd removed her gaze from him, the image of his powerful body seemed emblazoned on her mind's eye. Broad shoulders encased in a thin but soft wool sweater, the V-neck offering her a view of his strong, golden throat, collarbone and the barest hint of his upper chest. Jeans draped low on his hips and clung to the thick strength of his thighs. And his feet…bare.

This was the most relaxed she'd ever seen him, and that he'd allow her to glimpse him this way…it created an intimacy between them she resented and, God, foolishly craved. Because as silly as the presumption might be, she had a feeling he didn't unarm himself like this around many people.

Remember why you're here, her subconscious sniped. *Blackmail and coercion, not because you belong.*

"Did you want a sandwich?" she offered, the reminder shoring up any chinks in her guard.

"Thank you. It looks good." He moved farther into the room and withdrew one of the stools lining the island. Sitting down across from her, he nabbed the bread bin—because what else would one store freshly baked bread in?—and cut two thick slices while she returned to the refrigerator for more meat and cheese. "I'm sorry I had to leave earlier. I didn't want to miss Aiden's first night in the house. There was a bit of an emergency at the office."

"On a Saturday?" she asked, glancing at him.

He shook his head, the corner of his mouth quirking in a rueful smile. “When you’re the CEO and president of the company, there’s no such thing as a Saturday. Every day is a workday.”

“If you let it be,” she said. But then again, she understood the need to work when it called. As a single mom with more bills than funds, she hadn’t been able to turn down a shift at the supermarket or tell her mom she would skip helping her clean a house.

“True,” he agreed, accepting the ham she handed him. “But then I’ve never had a reason to dial back on the work. I do now,” he murmured.

Aiden. He meant Aiden and being a stepfather. She silently repeated the words to herself. But they didn’t prevent the warm fluttering in her belly or the hitch in her breath.

“How old are you?” she blurted out, desperate to distract herself from the completely inappropriate and stupid heat that pooled south of her belly button. “I don’t mean to be rude, but you don’t seem old enough to run a company.”

“Thirty,” he replied. She could feel his weighty gaze on her face like a physical touch as she finished preparing his meal. “My grandfather started the business as one corporation, and my father grew it into several corporations, eventually folding them all under one parent company. When he died, my father left King Industries Unlimited to me, and I started working there when I was seventeen, in the mail room. I went from there to retail sales associate to account manager and through the ranks, learning the business. By the time

I stepped in as CEO and president at twenty-five, and with the guidance of Baron, I had been an employee for seven years."

"Wow," she breathed. "Many men would've just assumed that position as their due and wouldn't bother with starting from the bottom." She hesitated, but then whispered, "I can only imagine your father would've been proud of your work ethic."

With his amber eyes gleaming, Darius nodded. "I hope so. It's how he did it, and I followed in his footsteps."

Their gazes connected, and the breath stuttered in her lungs. Her pulse jammed out an erratic beat at her neck and in her head.

Clearing her throat, she dropped her attention to her sandwich, and with more effort than it required, sliced it in half and did the same to his. "Tell me more about your work?" she requested, cursing the slight waver in her voice. Her biggest mistake would be letting Darius know he affected her in any manner. *Get it together, woman*, she scolded herself. "Was it hard suddenly running such a huge company?"

Over ham-and-cheese sandwiches, they spoke about his job and all it required. Eventually the conversation curved into more personal topics. He shared that his home had been his parents', one they'd purchased only months before they'd died. And the pocket watch collection had been his father's, and like the family company, Darius had taken it over and continued to add to it. She told him about her family, leaving out the part about her brother's lucrative but illegal side business.

Even her mother pretended it didn't exist and refused to accept any money earned from it. Isobel also added amusing stories about Aiden from the last two years.

"He took one look at Santa and let out the loudest, most terrified scream. I think the old guy damn near had a heart attack." She chuckled, remembering her baby's reaction to the mall Santa. "He started squirming and kicking his legs. His foot caught good ol' Saint Nick right in the boys, and they had to shut down Winter Wonderland for a half hour while, I'm sure, Santa iced himself in his workshop."

Darius laughed, the loud bark echoing in the room. He shook his head, shoulders shaking. His eyes, bright with humor, crinkled at the corners, and his smile lit up his normally serious expression.

An unsmiling Darius was devastatingly handsome.

A smiling Darius? Beyond description.

Slowly, as they continued to meet each other's gazes, the lightness in the room dimmed, converting into something weightier, darker. A thickness—congested with memories, things better left unspoken and desire—gathered between them. Even though her mind screamed caution, she didn't—couldn't—glance away. And if she were brutally honest? She didn't want to.

"You're different from how I remember you," he said, his gaze roaming over her face. Her lips prickled when that intense regard fell on her mouth and hovered for several heated moments. "Even though it was only a couple of times, you were quieter then, maybe even a little timid and withdrawn. At least around me. Gage said you were different around your family."

"I trusted them." She knew they wouldn't mock her just because she didn't use the proper fork or couldn't discuss politics. They accepted her, loved her. She'd never feared them.

Darius frowned, leaning forward on the crossed arms he'd propped on the marble island. "You didn't trust your husband?"

She paused, indecision about how much to share temporarily muting her. But, in the end, she refused to lie. "No," she admitted, the ghostly remnants of hurt from that time in her life rasping her voice. "I didn't."

How could she? Gage had been a liar, and he'd betrayed their short marriage. He'd promised her Harry and Meghan and had given her Henry VIII and wives one, two and five.

To gain his family's sympathy after marrying Isobel, he'd thrown her under the proverbial bus, accusing her of tricking him into marrying her by claiming she'd been pregnant. She hadn't been, though it'd happened shortly after their marriage. At first, they'd been happy—or at least she'd believed they'd been. True, they'd lived in a tiny apartment, living off her small paycheck from the grocery store while he looked for work since his family had cut him off, but they'd loved one another. After she'd refused to take a paternity test at the demand of his parents, things had changed. Subtly, at first, he'd isolated her from family and friends. He'd claimed that since his family had disowned him, it was just the two of them—soon to be the three of them—against the world. But that world had become smaller, darker, lonelier...scarier.

Gage had been a master gaslighter. Unknown to her, he'd thrown himself on his parents' mercies, spewing lies—that she'd demanded he abandon his family, that she was cheating on him. All to remain in the family fold as their golden child and maintain their compassion and empathy by making Isobel out to be a treacherous bitch he couldn't divorce and turn back out on the street. In truth, he'd been a spoiled, out-of-control child who hadn't wanted her but didn't want anyone else to have her either.

"He was your husband," Darius said, his tone as low as the shadows already accumulating in his eyes.

"He was my jailor," she snapped.

"Just like this is a prison?" he growled, sweeping a hand to encompass the kitchen, the beautiful home. "He gave you everything, while giving up his own family, his friends—hell, his world—for you. What more could he have possibly done to make you happy?"

Pain and anger clashed inside her, eating away any trace of the calm and enjoyment she'd found with Darius during the past hour. "Kindness. Compassion. Loyalty. Fidelity."

"It's convenient that he isn't here to defend himself, isn't it? Still, it's hard to play the victim now when we all know how you betrayed him, made a fool of him. In spite of all that, he wouldn't walk away from you." Fire flared in his eyes. The same fierce emotion incinerating her, hardened his full lips into a grim line. "I saw him just before he died. I begged him to walk away, to leave you. But he wouldn't. Even as it broke him that he couldn't even claim his son because of the men you'd fucked behind his back."

Trembling, Isobel stood, the scratch of the stool's legs across the tiled floor a discordant screech. Flattening her palms on the counter, she glared at him, in this moment, hating him.

"I broke him? He broke me! And destroyed whatever love I still had for him when he looked at our baby and called him a bastard. So don't you dare talk to me about being ungrateful. You don't know what the hell you're talking about."

Refusing to remain and accept any more accusations, she whipped around the island and stalked toward the kitchen entrance. Screw him. He didn't know her, had no clue—

"Damn it, Isobel," he snapped, seconds before his fingers wrapped around her upper arm.

"Don't touch—" She whirled back around and, misjudging how close he stood behind her, slammed into the solid wall of his chest. Her hands shot up in an instinctive attempt to prevent the tumble backward, but the hard band of his arms wrapped around her saved her from falling onto her ass.

The moment her body collided with his, the protest died on her tongue. Desire—unwanted, uncontrollable and greedy—swamped her. Her fingers curled into his sweater in an instinctive attempt to hold on to the only solid thing in a world that had constricted then yawned endlessly wide, leaving her dangling over a crumbling edge.

"Isobel." Her name, uttered in that sin-on-the-rocks

voice, rumbled through her, and she shook her head, refusing to acknowledge it—or the eruption of electrical pulses that raced up and down her spine. "Look at me."

His long fingers slid up her back, over her nape and tunneled into her hair. She groaned, unable to trap the betraying sound. Not when his hand tangled in the strands, tugging her head backward, sending tiny prickles along her scalp. She sank her teeth into her bottom lip, locking down on another embarrassing sound of pleasure.

"No," he growled, pressing his thumb to the center of her abused lip and freeing it. With a low, carnal hum, he rubbed a caress over the flesh. "Don't hold back from me. Let me hear what I do to you."

Oh, God. If she could ease her grip on his shirt, she'd clap her palms over her ears to block out his words. She hadn't forgotten how his voice had aided and abetted his touch in unraveling every one of her inhibitions the night of the blackout. It was a velvet weapon, one that slipped beneath her skin, her steel-encased guards, to wreak sensual havoc.

"Look at me, sweetheart," he ordered again. This time she complied, lifting her lashes to meet his golden gaze. "Good," he murmured, giving her bottom lip one last sweep with his fingers before burying them in her hair so both hands cupped her head. "Keep those fairy eyes on me."

Fairy eyes.

The description, so unlike him and so reminiscent of the man in the dark hallway weeks ago, swept over her like a soft spring rain. And then she ceased to think.

Because he proceeded to devastate her.

If their first kiss in the dark weeks ago started as a gentle exploration, this one was fierce. His mouth claimed and conquered, his tongue demanding an entrance she willingly surrendered. Wild and raw, he devoured her like a starving man intent on satisfying a bottomless craving. Again and again, he sucked, lapped, dueled, demanding she enter into carnal battle with him.

Submit to him. Take him. Dominate him.

With a needy whimper that should probably have mortified her, she fisted his shirt harder and rose on her toes, granting him even more access and commanding more of him. Angling her head, she opened her mouth wider, savoring his unique flavor, getting drunk on it.

But it wasn't enough. Never enough.

"Jesus Christ," he swore against her lips, nipping the lower curve, then pressing stinging kisses along her jaw and down her throat.

Kisses that echoed in her breasts, sensitizing them, tightening the tips. Kisses that eddied and swirled low in her belly. Kisses that had her thighs squeezing to contain the ache between her legs. Already a nagging emptiness stretched wide in her sex, begging to be filled by his fingers, his cock. Didn't matter. Just as long as some part of him was inside her, branding her.

The thought snuck under the desire, and once it infiltrated, she couldn't eject it. Instead it rebounded against her skull, loud and aggressive. *Branding me. Branding me.*

And Darius would do it; he would imprint himself into her skin, her body until she couldn't erase him from her thoughts...her heart. Until he slowly took over, and she ceased to exist except for the sole purpose of pleasing him...of loving him.

No. No, damn it.

Never again would she allow that to happen.

With a muted cry, she shoved her palms against his chest, lunging out of his embrace, away from his kiss, his touch.

Their harsh, jagged breaths reverberated in the kitchen. His broad chest rose and fell, his piercing gaze narrowed on her like that of a bird of prey's, waiting for her to make the slightest move so he could swoop in and capture her.

Even as her brain yelled at her to get the hell out of there, her body urged her to let herself be caught and devoured.

"No," she whispered, but not to him, to her traitorous libido.

"Then you better go," Darius ground out as if she'd spoken to him. *"Now."*

Not waiting for another warning, she whipped around, raced down the hall and bounded up the stairs. Once she closed the bedroom door behind her, she stumbled across the floor and sank to the mattress.

Oh, God, what had she done?

The no-sex rule had been hers. And yet the first time he'd touched her, she'd burned faster than kindling in a campfire.

Desire and passion were the gateways to losing reason, control and, eventually, independence.

Those who forget the past are condemned to repeat it.

She'd heard the quote many times throughout her life. But never had it been so true as this moment.

She'd made this one mistake.

She couldn't afford another.

Seven

An ugly sense of déjà vu settled over Isobel as she stared at the ornate front door of the Wellses' home. It'd been a slightly brisk October evening just like this one four years ago when she'd arrived on this doorstep, arm tucked in Gage's, excited and nervous to meet his family. She'd been so painfully naïve then, at twenty, never imaging the disdain she would experience once she crossed the threshold.

The differences between then and now could fill a hoarder's house. One, she was no longer that young girl so innocently in love. Second, she fully expected to be scorned and derided. And perhaps the most glaring change.

She stood next to Darius, but with Gage's son riding her hip.

Her stomach clenched, pulling into knots so snarled and tight, they would need Houdini himself to unravel them.

"There's no need to be nervous," Darius murmured beside her, settling a hand at the small of her back. The warmth of his hand penetrated the layers of her coat and dress, and she steeled herself against it, wishing he'd remove it. When about to enter the lion's den, she couldn't allow her focus and wits to be compromised by his touch. "I've already talked to them about us, and I'll be right here with you."

Was that supposed to be a reassurance? A pep talk? Well, both were epic fails. She wore no blinders when it came to Gage's family. Nothing—no talk or his presence—would ever convince them to accept her. She'd robbed them of their most precious gift. There was no forgiveness for that.

"This night is about Aiden," she said more to herself than him. "All I care about is how they treat him."

The weight of his stare stroked her face like the last rays of the rapidly sinking sun. She kept her attention trained on the door. It'd been almost a week since she'd moved into his home—since the night they'd kissed. And in that time, she'd become a master of avoidance. With a house the size of a museum, it hadn't proven to be difficult. When he spent time with Aiden, she withdrew to her room. And when she couldn't evade him, she ensured Aiden remained a buffer between them. A little cowardly? Yes. But when engaged in a battle for her dignity and emotional sanity, the saying "by any means necessary" had become her motto.

"They'll love him," he replied, with certainty and determination ringing in his voice.

Before she could respond, the door opened and Gabriella, Gage's sister, stood in the entranceway. The beautiful, willowy brunette, who was a feminine version of her brother, smiled, stepping forward to press a kiss to Darius's cheek.

An unfamiliar and nasty emotion coiled and rattled in Isobel's chest. Her grip on Aiden tightened, while her vision sharpened on the other woman.

Whoa.

Isobel blinked. Sucked in a breath. What the hell was going on? No way could she actually be...*jealous*. Not by any stretch of the imagination did Darius belong to her. And even if in some realm with unicorns and rainbows where he was hers to claim, Gabriella was like a sister to him.

Get a grip.

If this overreaction heralded the evening's future, it promised to be a long one. Long and painful.

"It's about time you arrived," Gabriella said, laying a hand on his chest. "Mother and Dad are climbing the walls."

"Now, that I'd pay money to see," he drawled.

So would Isobel.

"Gabriella, you remember Isobel." Darius's hand slid higher, to the middle of her back, and just this once, she was thankful for it.

The other woman switched her focus from Darius to Isobel. Jade eyes so like her brother's met hers, the warmth that had greeted Darius replaced with ice. Isobel fought not to shiver under the chill. *She can't hurt you. No one in this house can hurt you*, Isobel reminded herself, repeating the mantra. Hoping it was true.

"Of course," Gabriella said, her tone even, polite. "Hello, Isobel." She shifted her gaze to Aiden, who hugged Isobel's neck, his face buried against her coat. Unsurprisingly, he had a thumb stuck firmly in his mouth. Isobel didn't blame him or remove it. Hell, she suddenly wanted to do the same. "And this must be Aiden."

"Yes, it is." Darius removed his hand from Isobel's back and reached around to stroke a hand down her son's curls. Curls that were the same nearly black shade as Gabriella's. "Aiden, can you say hi?"

Shyly, Aiden lifted his head and whispered, "Hi," giving Gabriella a small wave.

The other woman stared at the toddler, her lips forming a small O-shape. Moisture brightened her gaze, and she blinked rapidly. "Hi, Aiden," she whispered back. Drawing in an audible breath, she looked at Darius. "He looks like Gage."

Anger flared to life in Isobel's chest. She wanted to snap, *Of course he does*, but she swallowed it down. Yet she could do nothing about the flames still flickering inside her.

Part of her wanted to say screw this and demand Darius drive them home. But the other half—the half that wanted the Wells family's derision toward her regarding Aiden's paternity laid to rest—convinced her to remain in place. She still resented their rejection of her son, but if they were willing to meet her halfway so Aiden could know them, then she could try to let it go.

Try.

"Come in." Gabriella stepped backwards, waving them inside, her regard still fixed on Aiden.

Minutes later, with their coats turned over to a waiting maid, they all strode toward the back of the house and entered a small parlor. Helena, lovely and regal, was perched upon the champagne-colored settee like a queen surveying her subjects from her throne. And Baron occupied the largest armchair, his salt-and-pepper hair—more salt now than the last time she'd seen him—gleaming under the light thrown by a chandelier.

Their conversation ended when Gabriella appeared with Darius, Aiden and Isobel in tow. Slowly, Baron stood, and Isobel just managed to refrain from frowning. Though still tall and handsome, his frame seemed thinner, even a little more…fragile. And perhaps the most shocking change was that the hard, condemning expression that had been his norm when forced to share the air with her was not in attendance. By no means was his gaze welcoming, but it definitely didn't carry the harshness it formerly had.

But the censure his demeanor lacked, Helena's more than made up for. She rose as well, her scrutiny as frigid and sharp as an icicle. Her mouth formed a flat, disapproving line, and for a moment Isobel almost believed she'd stumbled back in time. Gage's mother had disliked her on sight, and like a fine wine, the dislike had only aged. Into hatred.

Suddenly Isobel's arms tightened around Aiden,

flooded with the need to shield him, protect him. And herself. He was her lodestone, reminding her that she was no longer that timid, impressionable girl from the past.

"Darius." Baron crossed the room, his hand extended. Darius clasped it, and they pulled each other close for a quick but loving embrace. Then the older man turned toward her, and even with his lack of animosity, she braced herself. "Isobel, welcome back to our home." He stretched his hand toward her, and after a brief hesitation, she accepted it, her heart pulsing in her throat. His grip squeezed around her fingers, rendering her speechless, the gesture the most warmth he'd ever shown her. "And this is Aiden."

Awe saturated his deep baritone, the same wonder that had filtered through his daughter's in the foyer. His nostrils flared, his fingers curling into his palms as if he fought the need to reach out and touch her son. Clearing his throat, Baron switched his gaze back to Isobel.

"He has your eyes, but his features… It's like looking at a baby picture of my son," he rasped. "May I…?" He held his arms out toward Aiden.

Nerves jingled in her belly, but the plea in the man's eyes trumped them. "Aiden? Do you want to go to Mr. Baron?" She loosened her grip on her son and tried to hand him, but the child clung harder to her as he shook his head. "I'm sorry," she murmured, feeling regret at the flash of disappointment and hurt in the man's gaze. "He's a little shy around new people."

"A shame," Gabriella murmured behind her.

Isobel stiffened, a stinging retort dancing on the tip of her tongue. But Darius interceded, tossing a quelling glance toward Gage's sister over his shoulder. With an arched eyebrow and open hands, he silently requested to take Aiden. Dipping her chin, she passed her son to Darius, who practically launched himself into the man's arms. Aiden popped his thumb back into his mouth, grinning at Darius around it.

"Well, how about that," Baron whispered. "He certainly seems to have taken to you."

Darius shrugged, sweeping a hand down Aiden's small back. "It doesn't take long for him to warm up. And once he does, he'll talk your ear off." He poked Aiden's rounded tummy, and the boy giggled.

The cheerful, innocent sound stole into Isobel's heart, as it'd had done from the very first time she'd heard it.

"I have to admit, he does resemble Gage," Helena said, appearing at her husband's side, studying Aiden. "Isobel." She nodded, before dismissing her and turning to Darius, an affectionate smile thawing her expression. "Darius." She tilted her head, and he brushed a kiss on her cheek. "I haven't seen you in days. But it seems you have time for everyone else." She tapped him playfully on the chest. "Beverly Sheldon told me how she saw you at the Livingstons' dinner party. And how Shelly Livingston couldn't seem to keep her hands to herself." Helena chuckled as if immensely amused by Shelly Livingston's grabby hands.

Isobel fought not to react to the first shot fired across the bow. It hadn't taken long at all. She thought Helena or Gabriella would've at least waited until after drinks before they got in the first dig, but apparently the "you're an interloper and don't belong, darling" portion of the evening had begun.

Yet her purpose—letting Isobel know that Darius had attended a social event without her on his arm, probably out of shame—had struck true. Which was as inane as that flash of jealousy with Gabriella. Pretending to be the newly engaged, loving couple hadn't been a part of their bargain. He could do as he wanted, escort whom he wanted, flirt with whom he wanted… sleep with whom he wanted. It didn't matter to her.

Liar.

Flipping her once again intrusive, know-it-all subconscious the middle finger, she shored up the walls surrounding her heart.

"Beverly Sheldon gossips too much and needs to find a hobby," Darius replied, frowning. "It was an impromptu business dinner, not a party, and I'm sure Shelly's fiancé, who also attended with her father, would've had some objections if she 'couldn't seem to keep her hands to herself.'"

Helena waved his explanation off with a flick of her fingers and another laugh. "Well, you're a handsome man, Darius. It's not surprising women flock to you."

"Helena," Baron said, a warning heavy in her name.

"Now, don't 'Helena' me, Baron." She tsked, brushing her husband's arm before strolling off toward the bar across the room. "Would anyone like a drink?"

Good God. This was going to be a really long evening.

"Have you decided on whether or not you'll acquire SouthernCare Insurance?" Baron asked Darius, reclining in his chair as one of the servants placed an entrée plate in front of him.

Isobel let the business talk float over her, as she had most of the discussions around the dinner table. If the topics weren't about business, then it was Helena and Gabriella speaking about people and events Isobel didn't know anything about, and neither woman had made the attempt to draw her into the conversation. Not that she minded. The less they said to each other, the better the chance of Isobel making it through this dinner without emotional injuries from their sly innuendoes.

Still, right now she envied her son. By the time dinner was ready to be served, Aiden had been nodding off in Darius's arms. He'd taken Aiden to one of the bedrooms and settled him in. Aiden had escaped this farce of a family dinner, but she hadn't been as lucky.

Mimicking Baron, Isobel shifted backward, granting the servant plenty of room to set down her plate of food. When she saw the food, she barely managed not to flinch. Prime rib, buttered asparagus and acorn squash.

Gage's favorite meal.

She lifted her head and met Helena's arctic gaze. So the choice hadn't been a coincidence. No, it'd been deliberate, and just another way to let Isobel know she hadn't been forgiven.

Nothing had been forgotten.

Message received.

Picking up her fork—the correct fork—and knife, Isobel prepared to eat the perfectly cooked meat that would undoubtedly taste like ash on her tongue.

"I was leaning toward yes before the trouble with

their vice president leaked." Darius paused, murmuring a "thank you" as a plate was set in front of him. "One of their employees came forward about long-time, systematic sexual harassment within the company, and their senior vice president of operations is one of the key perpetrators. No," he said, shaking his head, tone grim. "I won't have King Industries Unlimited tainted with that kind of behavior."

Unlike the rest of the conversation surrounding business, Darius's comment snagged her attention, surprising her so much, she blurted out, "You would really base your decision on that?"

Silence crackled in the room. In the quiet, her question seemed to bounce off the walls. Everyone stared at her, but she refused to cringe.

It was Darius's scrutiny she resolutely met, ignoring the others'. And in his eyes, she didn't spy irritation at her interruption. No, just the usual intensity that rendered her breathless.

"Of course. I don't condone it, and I won't be associated with any business or person who does. Every person under my employ or the umbrella of my company should have the expectation of safety and an environment free of intimidation."

"Your employees are lucky to work for you then," she murmured.

More and more companies were trying to change their policies and eliminate sexual harassment—or at least indulge in lip service about removing it. But the truth couldn't be denied—not everyone enjoyed that sense of fairness or security. Even at the supermarket, the supervisor didn't think anything of calling her honey or flirting with her, going so far as to occasionally say how "lucky" her man was. She'd never bothered to correct him, assuming if he knew she didn't have a "man" at home, the inappropriate behavior would only worsen.

That Darius would turn down what was most likely a multimillion-dollar deal because of his beliefs and out of consideration for those under him… It was admirable. Heroic.

"I like to hope so," he replied just as softly.

A sense of intimacy seemed to envelop them, and she couldn't tear her gaze away from his. Her breath stuttered in her lungs, her heart tap-dancing a quick tattoo at the heat in those golden depths.

"Of course his employees are fortunate," Gabriella interjected, shattering the illusion of connection. "Darius is a good man. He doesn't brag about it, but he's founded—and often single-handedly funded—several foundations that provide scholarships for foster children, housing for abused women coming out of shelters, and literacy and job-placement programs for under-privileged youth. And those are just some of his…projects."

The strategic pause before "projects" let Isobel know Gabriella considered *her* to be one of those charity cases. If passive-aggressiveness was a weapon, Gabriella and Helena would own codes and security clearances.

"It's wonderful to know Aiden will have an admirable role model in Darius," Isobel said, voice neutral.

Silence once more descended in the room, but Isobel didn't shrink from it. The scared, quiet girl they had known no longer existed; the woman she was now wouldn't stand mutely like a living target for their verbal darts.

Darius glanced at her, and once more she found herself trapped in his gaze. Something flickered in the golden depths. Something that had her lifting her glass of wine to her lips for a deep sip.

"If Gage couldn't be here to raise him, he would've wanted family to do it," Darius finally said to the room, but his eyes… His eyes never wavered from her.

"Still," Helena pressed, not looking at Darius but keeping her attention firmly locked on Isobel. "A boy should know his father. Tell me, Isobel, since you claim Aiden is Gage's, have you showed him pictures? Does he know who his real father is?"

"Helena," Darius growled a warning.

"Darius, darling," Helena replied, tilting her head to the side. "We all commend you for your sacrifice in this difficult situation, but I think you'd agree that a child deserves to know who his true parents are, right?"

A muscle jumped along Darius's jaw, but Isobel set her glass down on the table, meeting Helena's scrutiny.

"I've always shown Aiden pictures of Gage, since he is Aiden's father, as well as talked to him about Gage. And he understands who his *real father* is, as much as a two-year-old can."

"Hmm," came Helena's noncommittal, *condescending* answer.

"Aiden looks so much like Gage when he was that

age," Baron added from the head of the table, aiming a quelling glance at his wife.

But Helena didn't respond, instead turning to Gabriella and asking about a function she was supposed to attend that week.

Pain and humiliation slashed at Isobel, but she fought not to reveal it. Not only did she refuse to grant them that pleasure, but she didn't have anything to be ashamed of. They accused *her* of cheating, when the opposite had been true.

But what would be the point in trying to explain the truth to his family? They would never believe her. Not after they'd always accepted every utterance from Gage as the gospel.

And with him dead, he was even more of a saint.

And she would always be a sinner.

Eight

Darius poured himself another glass of bourbon. This would be his third. Or maybe fourth. Didn't matter. He wasn't drunk yet; he could still think. So whatever number he was on, it wouldn't be his last. He'd keep tossing it back until the unease and anger no longer crawled inside him like ants in a colony.

Tonight had been a clusterfuck. Oh, it'd been frigidly polite, but still… Clusterfuck.

After crossing the study, he sank down onto the couch and took a sip of the bourbon. Clasping the squat glass, he slid down, resting his head on the couch's back, his legs sprawled wide.

Jesus, when would the forgetful part of this begin?

He hated this sense of…betrayal that clung to him like a filthy film of dirt. And no matter how hard he tried to scrub it clean with excuses, it remained, stubborn and just as grimy.

When he'd asked Isobel to the Wellses' house that night, he'd promised her they would be civil, and she would be in a safe space, be welcomed. Baron had, but Helena and Gabriella, they'd made a liar of him. He understood their resentment—even now, when he thought of Gage, that mixture of anger and grief still churned in his chest, his gut. But tonight had been about Aiden, about them connecting with the boy, and that meant forging a fragile truce with his mother. Showing her respect, at least.

Hours later, the disappointment, the disquiet continued to pulse within him like a wound, one that refused to heal.

Isobel had definitely been enemy number one when she'd been married to Gage. All of them believed Gage had moved too fast, married too young. Darius had been equally confused when he'd cut them all off for almost a year. None of them could understand why Gage hadn't divorced her, especially when he started confiding in them about her infidelity. As far as Darius could tell, his friend had genuinely been in love with his wife, and her betrayals had destroyed him.

Still. Remembering the woman he'd shared a hallway with in the dark… The woman who loved her son so selflessly… The woman whose family rallied around her, supported her and her son unconditionally… That Isobel didn't really coincide with the one the Wellses detested.

But if he were brutally honest—and alcohol had a

way of dragging that kind of truth forth—it hadn't only been this evening that had unnerved him.

She did.

Everything about her unsettled him.

From the thick dark hair with the hints of fire to the delectable, curvaceous body that tempted him like a red flag snapping in front of a bull.

Earlier, when she'd thrust her chin up in that defiant angle, he'd had to force himself to remain in his seat instead of marching around the table and shocking the hell out of everyone by tugging her head back and claiming that beautiful, created-for-sin mouth.

Another truth he could admit in the dark with only bourbon for company.

He wanted her.

Fuck, did he want her.

Maybe if the past had stayed in the past, he could have convinced himself their space of time in the hallway had been just that—a blip, an anomaly. But once he'd kissed her again, once he'd swallowed her moans, once he'd felt her slick, satiny flesh spasm around his fingers as she came… No, he craved this woman with a need that was usually reserved for oxygen and water.

Even knowing that she'd betrayed Gage just as Faith had cheated on Darius, he still couldn't expunge this insane, insatiable desire.

So, what did that say about him? About his dignity? His fucking intelligence?

He snorted, raising his glass to his lips for a deep sip.

It said that, as much as he'd claimed to the contrary, his dick had equal partnership with his brain.

Yet…he frowned into the golden depths of the bourbon. The more time he spent with Isobel, the more doubt crept into his head, infiltrating his long-held ideas about her, about the woman he'd believed her to be. But for him to accept that she was not the woman who'd betrayed her husband in the past, it would mean that Gage had consciously—and maliciously—lied to Darius's face. And to his family. And to all of their friends. It would mean Darius's best friend, the man who'd been closer to him than a brother, had intentionally destroyed Isobel's reputation.

And that he couldn't believe.

Could Gage have somehow misinterpreted her actions? Or maybe there was more to the story that Gage hadn't shared with his family before his death?

"Darius?"

He glanced in the direction of the study's entrance, where the sound of his name in *her* voice had originated.

And immediately wished he hadn't.

Now the image of her standing in the doorway, barefoot, her long, toned legs exposed by some kind of T-shirt that hit her midthigh, and hair a sexy tumble around her beautiful face would be permanently branded onto his retinas.

"What are you wearing?" he growled.

Hell, he hadn't intended to vocalize that question. And with his bourbon-weakened control, no way in hell could he prevent the lust careering through him.

She peeked down at herself, then returned her fairy eyes to him. "What?" she asked. "This is what I sleep in. Excuse me if it's not La Perla enough for you, but I didn't exactly expect to bump into anyone."

La Perla. Fox and Rose. Agent Provocateur.

His ex-wife had insisted on only purchasing the expensive, luxury lingerie for herself, and they'd shown up regularly on his credit card statements, which was the only reason he recognized the brands.

But damn. Now, staring at her body with those lethal curves, he would love to put that useless-until-now information to work. To drape her in the softest silk and the most delicate lace. To personally choose corsets, bras and panties to adorn a woman who didn't need anything to enhance her ethereal beauty and earthy sensuality. And still he wanted to give them to her. To see her in them.

To peel them from her.

Taking another sip, he wrenched his gaze from the temptation in cotton.

"What do you want, Isobel?" he rasped.

She stepped into the room, the movement hesitant. It should be. If she had any idea of the need grinding inside him like a relentlessly turning screw, she'd leave.

"I was headed toward the kitchen and saw the light on in here. I thought you'd gone to bed." A pause. "Are you okay?"

"I'm fine," he said automatically. *Lie.*

"I'm sorry for you," she said, gliding farther into the room and halting a small distance from him. As if unsure whether or not she should chance come any closer.

Smart woman.

The way the alcohol and lust coursed through him

like rain-swollen rapids, he should warn her away, bark an order to get out of the study. Instead he watched her, a predator silently waiting for his prey to approach just near enough for him to pounce.

"Sorry for me," he repeated on a serrated huff of laughter. "Why?"

"Because I went there tonight knowing I wouldn't be welcome. I wasn't surprised by anything that happened. But you were shocked…and hurt. And for that, I'm sorry."

He lifted his head, stared at her, astonishment momentarily robbing him of speech.

Discomfort flickered across her features, and she shrugged a shoulder. "Anyway… Your relationship with them isn't my business…"

"You weren't hurt?" He ground his teeth around a curse. He hadn't intended to snap at her. Dragging in a deep breath, he held it, then exhaled. "You weren't hurt by what they said, how they acted?"

She studied him for a long second, then slowly shook her head. "No, Darius. For me, it was business as usual. For the two years I was married, I was never good enough. Smart enough. Sophisticated enough. Just never…enough."

"I can't believe that," he snapped, banging his glass on the table and surging to his feet. Tunneling his fingers through his hair, he paced away from her. He *couldn't.* Because then what did that say about the past, about what he'd believed?

What would it say about the family he idolized?

"It's not that you can't believe it. You won't," she

contradicted, her voice low, laced with an unmistakable thread of resignation. As if she hadn't expected much from him. Certainly not for him to accept her truth. "And you never will. You won't allow yourself to even consider that the brave man who saved you from a burning building, the honorable man who became your brother when you lost your parents could've changed. Or at the very least, had one side with you and another with his wife, who he grew to resent almost from the moment he said 'I do.'"

"No," Darius rasped, stalking closer and eliminating the small space between them. "He went against his family's wishes to have you, risking everything for you…"

"And he came to hate me for it," she whispered, tilting her head back to meet his gaze. "Just like you eventually will. You said you're going through with this engagement and marriage for Baron, Helena and Gabriella. What happens when they force you to choose between your pretend wife and them? Because it'll happen. They've earned your love, your loyalty, but you've given your word to me. Oh, yes." She nodded, shadows swirling in her lovely, haunted eyes. "In the end, you'll resent me, too."

He squeezed his eyes closed, his jaw so hardened, so tense, the muscles along it twinged. Emotion. So much emotion howled and whistled inside him, he feared one misstep, one wrong-placed touch, and he would shred under the power of it.

"I already resent you, Isobel," he ground out, forcing himself to meet her gaze. Her scent—delicate like newly opened rose petals and intoxicating like the bourbon he'd been drinking—wrapped around him with phantom arms. Heat emanated from her petite body, and he wanted to curl against it. "And it has nothing to do with tonight or a future emotional tug-of-war. I hate that I can't get you out of my head. Can't stop replaying a night that should've never happened. I can still *feel* you. Your lips parting for mine. Your skin under my hands. Your tight, soaking-wet flesh gripping my fingers so hard, it almost bruised me. You just won't get out of my goddamn head."

Lust churned his voice to the consistency of gravel. "I hate that I know who you are, and I still want to fuck you. I hate that I can't tell if you're the sweet, giving woman from that dark hallway or the conniving one who was married to my best friend." He shifted that scant inch forward and brought his chest to hers, his thighs to hers. His breath to hers. "I hate that I want to find out."

Her labored pants broke across his mouth, and he slicked his tongue across his lips, seeking to taste that hard puff of breath. Her scrutiny followed the movement, and like clouds moving in over a blue sky, lust darkened her gaze. God, why didn't she close those beautiful eyes? Shield both of them from the knowledge that she craved him as he did her? He placed the responsibility on her, because he was the weaker one. She had to be the strong one and save them both.

"Turn around and walk out of here, Isobel," he warned her, his voice so guttural, he almost winced. "I'll break your condition. I'll put my hands and mouth on you. I'll finish what we started in the dark if you don't."

A small, muted whimper escaped her. Almost as if she'd tried to trap the needy sound but hadn't been fast enough.

"You're not running, sweetheart." He lifted his hand, let it hover over her cheek for a weighty moment, granting her time to evade it. But she remained still, and he swept the pad of his thumb over her cheekbone, then lower, across the lush curve of her bottom lip.

"No," she whispered. "I'm not."

"Your rule," he whispered back.

"Break it… Break me."

The request, uttered on a trembling breath, snapped the already tattered ropes on his control, and with a groan, he crushed his mouth to hers. When her heady taste hit his tongue, that groan morphed into a growl. Delicious. Addictive. He drove his fingers into her hair, tipping her head back so he could gorge on her. Yeah, he was committing the sin of gluttony, and resigned himself to hell for it.

Her palms slid over his sides and up his back, curling into the backs of his shoulders. The bite of her nails sent pleasure sizzling through him like an electrical charge, arrowing straight for his cock. He shifted, pressing harder against her, giving her full, undeniable disclosure to what she did to him.

Abandoning her hair, he dropped his arms, molding his hands to her ass, cupping the curves. He bent his knees, then abruptly straightened, hiking her into his arms. A bolt of carnal satisfaction struck him when her legs wrapped around his waist and her arms encircled his neck, holding on to him. Her mouth clung to his, that wicked tongue twisting and tangling, dancing and dueling. Damn, he wanted that talented mouth on his skin, on every part of him.

After quickly striding back to the couch, he sank down to the cushions, arranging her so she straddled his thighs. He broke their kiss long enough to fist the hem of her shirt and yank it over her head. All that hair tumbled down around her shoulders, back and chest, transforming her into a seductive siren. He wanted to crash himself against her and drown in pleasure.

"You're going to take me under, aren't you?" he murmured, voicing his thoughts.

"Are you afraid?" she asked.

He shifted his enraptured gaze from her hair to her eyes.

Yes.

The reply erupted inside him, ringing with certainty, but he didn't vocalize it. Instead he cradled the nape of her neck and drew her forward until their lips brushed, pressed, mated.

Impatient, he stroked a caress over her shoulders, down her chest and finally reacquainted himself with the flesh he'd dreamed about before waking up, hard and hurting. He cupped her, squeezed…and it wasn't enough. Ripping his mouth free of hers, he bent his head, trailed his lips over the soft swell of her breast, then circled his tongue around the taut, dusky peak.

Her cry rebounded off the walls and windows, and her arms clasped him to her. Her scent, rich and deep, filled his nostrils, and he licked it off her skin. In response, her hips rolled, rocking her lace-covered folds over him. The pressure against his erection had him hauling in a breath and bracing himself against the stunning pleasure barreling through him. He shifted beneath her, sliding down a fraction so his length notched firmly against her. He dropped a hand to her hip, encouraging her to continue riding him. Continue stoking the fire between them until it consumed them.

"You're so sweet." He lapped at her nipple, then drew it into his mouth, suckling on her, tormenting her as she was doing to him. "Dangerous," he admitted.

Her only response was to buck those slim hips. It was the only response he needed. Switching to her neglected breast, he worshipped it, losing himself in the taste, texture and wonder of her.

"Let me," she panted, gripping his hair and tugging his head up. He resisted, but spying her flushed cheeks, swollen lips and glazed eyes, he relented. "I want to… need to…"

She didn't finish the thought, but with trembling fingers, plucked at his shirt buttons. Too impatient, he replaced her attempt with a hard yank. The buttons flew, scattered, and he tore off the offensive material.

"God," she breathed, flattening her palms to his chest. He shuddered, the sensation of being skin to skin almost too sharp. "You're beautiful. So…beautiful."

Another shiver rippled through him, just as intense, but it was the result of her words rather than her touch. Or rather the stark truth in her words. When they were clothed, minds and bodies not warped by passion, he didn't trust her. But here…with their bodies stripped… honesty existed between them. The honesty of lust and pleasure. She couldn't hide from him, couldn't lie to him. Not when the evidence of her desire soaked her underwear and his pants.

He loosened a hand from the soft ropes of her hair and slid it down her back, over her hip and between her legs. She stiffened a second, and he paused, imprisoning a groan as her wet heat singed him. But only when she melted against him, her whispered, "Please" granting him permission to continue, did he slip underneath the plain but sexy-as-hell underwear to the soft, plush flesh beneath.

She jerked, whimpered as he glided through the path created by her folds, ending his journey with a firm circle over her clit. The little bundle of nerves contracted and pulsed under his fingertip, and he teased it. She straightened, her hands clutching at his shoulders, her back arched, surrendering to his touch.

She was the most goddamn beautiful thing he'd ever seen.

"I love how wet you get for me," he rasped, stroking her hair away from her face, studying her pleasure-stricken expression. Dipping his hand lower, he rimmed her tiny, fluttering entrance. "You have more for me, sweetheart?"

He didn't wait for a reply but drove a finger inside her. Her cry caressed his ears even as her silken sex clutched at him, convulsed around him. He growled, loving her response to him. Hungry for more. Withdrawing, he slid in another finger, stretching her, preparing her to take him so he wouldn't inadvertently hurt her. And the selfish side of him reveled in the tight clasp of her body, in the soft undulations of her flesh that relayed her pleasure and impatience. Impatience for him, for what he was giving her. For what he was promising her.

"Can you take another?" he murmured, pulling free again.

"Yes." Her fingernails denting his skin. "Please, yes."

Leaning forward, he opened his mouth over the pulse throbbing like a snare drum at the base of her throat as he slowly buried three fingers inside her. She bucked her hips, twisting like a wild thing on his lap. Jesus, she was gorgeous in passion—sexy, uninhibited and burning like a blue flame. Her desire scorched him.

Grinding out a curse, he lifted her off his thighs and set her beside him. Ignoring her disappointed cry, he shed her of the underwear, leaving her bare before him. With his gaze fixed on her lovely nakedness, he removed his wallet from his pants. Then he snatched out a condom and shoved his pants down his legs, too desperate to be inside her to completely strip them off.

With hands he prayed were gentler than the maelstrom of greed tearing at him, he repositioned her over him. He couldn't prevent the shiver that worked its way through him as he fisted the base of his cock, notching the tip at the entrance to her body. Perspiration trickled down his skin as he slowly—so damn slowly—lowered her over him.

God. Every muscle in his body tightened, with the

control it required not to plunge himself inside exacting its toll.

Hot.

Tight.

Ecstasy.

Fire raced up and down his spine, snapping and crackling. It rolled and thundered through his veins, transforming his blood to pure, undiluted pleasure. Already she consumed him, and he hadn't even seated himself fully inside her. And though razor-sharp need sliced at him, he didn't rush it. He'd rather suffer before hurting Isobel. Even now those tiny muscles rippled and fluttered over his flesh, adjusting to his penetration. Tremors quaked through her petite frame, and whimpers slipped past her lips.

"Shh," he soothed, pausing. Keeping one hand braced on her hip, he cupped her cheek with the other, tipping her head down. "Your pace, sweetheart. Tell me what you need, and it's yours," he said against her lips.

"Kiss me."

She tilted her head, opening for him, and he twisted his tongue with hers, sucking on it. She joined in the duel, thrusting and parrying. Pursuing and eluding. It turned wild, raw.

Before the kiss ended, she sat fully and firmly on his cock.

With a snarl, he tore away from her, tipping his head back against the couch. She was…perfect.

"Isobel," he growled, raising his head again, unable to *not* see what she did to him. How she took him.

Cradling her hips, he lifted her, stared in rapt fascination as she unsheathed him, leaving his length glistening with the evidence of her desire. Then when just the head remained inside her, he eased her back down, still watching as she parted for him, claiming him.

Branding him.

"After that night in the hallway," he gritted out, pulling free again. "I regretted not taking you. Not knowing how it felt to bury myself inside you. But now," he rasped, lowering her. "Now I'm glad I didn't. Because then I would've missing seeing how you so sweetly spread for me. And that, sweetheart...that would've been a crime."

"Darius," she whispered, and the sound of his name on her lips tattered the remnants of his control.

He drove inside her, snatching her down to him. Not that he needed to. She rode him, fierce and powerful, and in that moment, she was the one doing the claiming. And he surrendered, letting her incinerate him. And he held on, thrusting, giving, willingly being rendered to ash.

"Please," she begged, her body quaking. She clung to him even as she surged and writhed against him. "Please, Darius."

He didn't need her to complete the thought; he already knew what she wanted. Reaching between them, he stroked a path down her belly and between her legs. Murmuring, he rubbed the pad of his thumb over her swollen clit. Once. Twice...

Before he could reach three, her sex clamped down on him, a strangling, muscular vise that dragged a grunt out of him. She exploded, seizing his cock, spasming and pulsing around him as she flew apart in his arms.

He rode her through it, thrusting hard and quick, ensuring she received every measure of the release that gripped her. Only when the quakes eased into shivering did he let go.

Pleasure—powerful, intense and brutal—plowed into him. His brain shorted, his vision grayed as he threw himself into an orgasm like a willing sacrifice, wanting to be consumed, obliterated, reshaped.

But into what? The unknown terrified him.

Then, as the darkness submerged and swamped him, he didn't think.

Couldn't think.

Could only feel.

And then, not even that.

Nine

Isobel released a weary sigh as she pulled into an empty spot in the four-car garage.

Darius had moved one of his luxury vehicles so she could have a parking space, and had invited her to drive one of them. But she had yet to take him up on the offer. She'd already invaded his house, and she and Aiden were living off his money. Taking one of the cars as if she owned it edged her one step closer to being the gold-digging creature she'd been called. So no, she'd continued driving her beat-up but trusty Honda Civic. Even if parking it next to his Bugatti Chiron seemed like blasphemy.

Climbing out of her car, she inhaled the early evening air. Though she'd left work at the grocery store without wearing her jacket, she now drew it around her, the black collared shirt and khakis of her uniform not fighting off the nippy breeze.

Glancing down at her watch, she picked up her pace and strode toward the front door of Darius's home. It was just nearing five o'clock, and like the previous days, she was hoping she'd beat him home from work. Since she no longer had to work a second shift with her mother to make ends meet, she'd switched her hours at the store. Four days a week, she left the house at eight to arrive for her nine-to-four shift. Isobel liked the nanny, Ms. Jacobs, just fine. She was grateful for her, because her presence allowed Isobel to continue working even when she couldn't ask her mom to watch Aiden. Still, she missed her son fiercely when she left.

And yet over the last few days, she'd been thankful for her job. Concentrating on customers, price checks and sales prevented her from obsessively dwelling on... other things.

Other things being the cataclysmic event of sex with Darius.

A flush rushed up from her chest and throat, pouring into her face. She loosened her collar as the memories surged forth, as if they'd been hovering on the edges of her subconscious, waiting for the opportunity to flood her.

Her step faltered, and she stumbled. "Damn," she muttered.

No matter how many times those mental images flashed across her brain, they never failed to trip her up—literally and figuratively. She vacillated between cringing and combusting. Cringing at the thought of her completely abandoned and wild reaction to him.

Combusting as she easily—too easily—recalled how his mouth and hands had pleasured her, marked her. How he'd triggered a need in her that eclipsed any previous sexual experience, rendering all other men inconsequential and mediocre.

He'd spoiled her for anyone else.

And she'd committed a fatal error in letting him know just how much she craved him.

So yes, she'd been avoiding him, trying to reinforce her emotional battlements. And surprisingly he'd allowed her to evade him. The few times they'd been in the same room since That Night, he'd treated her with a distant politeness that both relieved and irritated her. Pretending as if they'd never shook in each other's arms, him buried inside her to the hilt.

Pinching the bridge of her nose as she entered the house, she deliberately slammed the door on those memories, and not just locked it but threw three dead bolts just for good measure.

"Where have you been?"

She skidded to a halt in the foyer at the furious demand, her head jerking up. Shock doused her in a frigid wave, and she stared at Darius. Anger glittered in his amber gaze, tightened the skin over his sharp cheekbones and firmed the full curve of his mouth into a flat line.

"Hello to you, too, Darius," she drawled with acid sweetness.

"Where. Have. You. Been?" he ground out, his big

body vibrating with emotion. It flared so bright in his eyes, they appeared like molten gold.

"At work, although I don't see how that's any of your business," she snapped. "Which is becoming a common refrain between us. I might be in your home, but no clause in that contract mandated me having to run my every movement by you."

A snarl curled the corner of his lips, and he shifted a step forward but stopped himself. "I beg to disagree with you on that, Isobel. When it has to do with Aiden's care and no one knows where the hell you've been for hours, and you don't answer your cell phone, then it most definitely. Is. My. Business." He pivoted away from her, the action sharp, full of anger. His fingers plowed through his hair, fisting it, before he turned back to her. "Aiden started coughing and became irritable, and when Ms. Jacobs took his temperature, he had a low-grade fever. She tried to call you to see if you wanted her to make a doctor's appointment for him. When she couldn't reach you, she called me. Damn it, Isobel," he growled. "I didn't know if something had happened to you or if you were in trouble or hurt..." Again, he glanced away from her, a muscle ticking along his clenched jaw. "No one could find you," he finally growled.

Worry for her son washed away her annoyance and propelled her forward. "Is he okay? I can take him to an after-hours clinic..."

"He's fine. I had a doctor come out and examine him. He has a virus, probably a twenty-four-hour bug, but nothing serious. I've just looked in on him, and he's sleeping."

Relief threaded through her concern, but didn't get rid of it. As a cashier, she wasn't allowed to have a cell phone on the floor. When her mother had been watching Aiden, this hadn't been a problem, as she'd trusted her mother to handle anything that came up. Not to mention that the store had been minutes from her mom's place. Maybe she should've given Darius her work schedule, or told him she was continuing to work at the store, period. And she'd just told Ms. Jacobs she was going to be out.

Damn. She turned toward the staircase, her thoughts already on her baby. But Darius's voice stopped her.

"I'll be in the library, Isobel. After you look in on him, come find me. This conversation isn't finished." The "don't make me come find you" was implicit in the order, but she ignored it, instead rushing up the stairs to her son.

Fifteen minutes later, after she'd satisfied herself that he was resting and breathing easily, she headed toward the library. Her heart thudded against her chest, her blood humming in her veins. Returning to the scene of the crime. She'd barely glanced at the entrance to the room since she'd last left it, and now she had to re-enter it. Maybe sit on the same couch where she'd lost her control, her pride and possibly her mind.

She hated having to enter this room again and be reminded of how she'd come apart. Of how she'd cemented his belief that she was an immoral whore who would screw anyone. After all, she'd claimed not to want him, but at his first touch, she'd surrendered.

Break it... Break me.

Hadn't those been the words she'd uttered as she begged him? *Break the no-sex rule she'd instituted. Break her with his passion.*

Briefly, she closed her eyes, attempting to smother the humiliation crawling into her throat, squatting there and strangling her.

Deliberately keeping her gaze off the couch, she strode into the room and located Darius, who was in front of his desk, with his arms crossed and his eagle-eyed scrutiny fixed on her.

"Isobel."

"Can we get this over with so I can return to Aiden?"

He didn't move, but she could practically *see* him bristle. "How is he?" he asked, surprising her once more with his concern for her son.

"Sleeping, as you said," she murmured. "He's still warm, but he seems to be resting okay." Drawing in a breath, she mimicked his pose, crossing her arms over her chest. "I'm sorry you couldn't reach me. That was my fault. I was at work, and management doesn't allow us to have our cells on us. And I didn't even notice I had missed calls when I left. So I apologize for worrying...everyone."

"Work?" he asked, his voice dropping to a low rumble. "What 'work'?"

"I'm sure the private investigator you hired included my job in his or her report," she said, sarcasm dripping from her tone. "If not, you might want to request a refund for his shoddy performance."

He shook his head, dropping his arms to slash a

hand through the air. "Don't tell me you're still going to that supermarket?"

"Of course I am," she replied. "That contract didn't require me to give up my job."

"Why?" he demanded. "You don't need the job, especially when it pays basically pennies. And yes, I do know how much you make, since my investigator's report included not only where you work but how much you're paid," he added.

"There's nothing wrong with ringing up groceries. It's good, honest work." She thrust her chin up. "Maybe you're so far removed from that time in the mail room, you don't remember what that's like."

"No, there's nothing wrong with your job." He frowned, cocking his head to the side. "But what do you need it for, Isobel? If there's something you want, why don't you just come to me and ask?"

His obvious confusion and—hurt?—smoothed out the ragged edges of her anger. How could she make him understand?

After his parents had died, he might've lived with the Wellses, but he'd never been totally dependent on them. Not with a multibillion-dollar empire waiting on him. Not with homes scattered around the country and money in bank accounts. He didn't know the powerlessness, the helplessness of being totally reliant on someone else's generosity…or lack of it.

She'd learned that particular lesson the hard way with Gage. Yes, she might've held down the job when she'd been married, but Gage had considered his role to be manager of their finances. And he'd been horribly irresponsible with them. And later, when his parents had parceled out sympathy money to him, he'd stingily doled that out to her, holding money for things like groceries and diapers over her head.

Never again would she be at the mercy of a man.

And if that meant keeping a low-paying job with good hours so she could maintain a measure of independence, then she would do what was necessary. If it meant losing some time with Aiden while she squirreled away her wages, well, then sacrifices needed to be made. She needed to be able to provide for them when Darius's charity finally reached its limits.

She was a mother first. And any good mother did what needed to be done.

"Then enlighten me, Isobel. Because I don't understand. You have a home. You don't have to pay any bills. You even have cars at your disposal if you'd stop being so damn prideful and use them—"

"No, you're wrong," she interrupted, her voice quiet but heavy with the emotion pressing against her sternum. Frustration, irritation and sadness. "*You* have a home. *You* have cars at your disposal. *Your* money pays the bills. None of this is mine. Even after we sign that marriage certificate and exchange vows, it still won't be. If you put me out, I couldn't leave with any of it. Couldn't lay claim to it. And you could put me out at any time, on any whim, because of any conceived sin on my part. And I would be on the street, homeless, with no money or resources for me and my son. No." She shook her head. "I won't allow that to happen."

He stared at her, shock darkening his eyes. His lips

parted, head jerking as if her words had delivered a verbal punch.

"I would never abandon you or Aiden like that," he said, the words uttered like a vow.

She knew only too well how vows could be broken.

"I know you believe you wouldn't. But minds change, feelings change," she murmured. Then, suddenly feeling so tired that her limbs seemed to weigh a hundred pounds, she sighed, pinching the bridge of her nose. "Are we done here? I need to get back to Aiden."

"No," he said, the denial firm, adamant. As if it'd pushed through a throat coated in broken glass. "You don't believe me."

"I wanted to return to college. Did you know that?" she asked softly. Without waiting for him to reply, she continued, "One of my regrets is that I quit school. I would've been the first one in my family to earn a degree if I'd stayed. So graduating from college was a dream of mine, but when I broached it with Gage, he convinced me to wait until after the baby was born. At the time, I thought him wanting that time for the two of us was sweet. So I agreed. But after Aiden came, I couldn't go back. Working a full-time job, being a mom..." She shrugged. "College would've been too much, so I had to place it on the back burner. But I've always wanted to go back. To obtain that degree. To have a career that I love. And when Aiden is older, I'll show him that no matter how you struggle, you can do anything you desire."

Scrubbing her hands up and down her arms, she paced to the wide floor-to-ceiling window and stared sightlessly at the view of his Olympic-size pool, deck and firepit. Her admission made her feel vulnerable, exposed.

"Did Gage support your dream?" Darius asked quietly.

She didn't turn around and face him. Didn't let him see the pain and anger she couldn't hide. Darius didn't want to hear the truth. Wasn't ready to hear it. And he wouldn't believe her anyway. College, money for tuition—those had been givens in his and Gage's worlds. He wouldn't understand or see how his friend would begrudge his wife that same experience.

"Gage had specific ideas about the wife he wanted," she whispered instead. "A wife like his mother." One to cater to him. Be at his beck and call. Place him as the center of her universe, at the exclusion of everyone else.

Images from that time flashed across her mind, and she deliberately shut them down, refusing to tumble back into that dark time when she'd been so helpless and powerless.

Silence descended on the room, and she swore she could feel Darius's confusion and disbelief pushing against her.

"If what you say is true, how—"

She'd expected him not to believe her. But she *hadn't* expected the dagger-sharp pain to slice into her heart. Uttering a sound that was somewhere between a scoff and a whimper, she turned, unable to stand there while he doubted every word that came out of her mouth. This is what she got for opening up and letting him in even a little.

Lesson learned.

"Wait. *Damn it, Isobel,*" he growled, his arms wrapping around her, his chest pressing to her spine. His hold, while firm, wasn't constrictive, and it was this fact that halted her midescape. "That came out wrong. Just give me a minute. Don't I have the right to ask questions? To try to understand?"

A pause—where the only sound in the room was the echo of their harsh breaths. He loosened his arms, releasing her and taking his warmth with him. Turbulent emotions surged up from the place deep inside her that remained wounded and bruised. The place that cried out like a heartsore child for satisfaction, for someone to hear her, for acceptance. That place urged her to lash out, to hurt as she'd been hurt.

But flashes of Darius being so affectionate with Aiden, of him upset on her behalf after the dinner with the Wellses, of him kissing and touching her—those flashes filled her head. And it was those flashes that tempered her reply.

"Love blinds us all."

Unable to say any more, unable to hear him defend his friend and family, she left the study and climbed the stairs to return to Aiden.

How they could ever forge a peaceful, if not loving, marriage when the past continued to intrude?

And to that question, she didn't have an answer.

Ten

"No, Mommy!"

Darius heard Aiden's strident, high-pitched objection before he stepped into the doorway of the boy's room. Isobel sat on one of the large beanbag chairs, Aiden curled on her lap, reading a book. Well, Isobel was reading anyway, Darius mused, humor bubbling inside him.

"No," Aiden yelled again, stabbing a chubby finger at one of the pages. "Nose." He twisted around and declared, "Eye," nearly taking out hers with his enthusiastic poke. "Nose," he repeated, squishing his with the same finger.

Isobel laughed, dropping a kiss on his abused nose. "You're right, baby. Nose. Good job!"

"Good job," he mimicked, clapping.

Warmth slid through Darius's veins like liquid sun. The previous evening had left him confused, and the maddening cacophony of questions lingered.

Gage had specific ideas about the wife he wanted.

She'd made it sound like she hadn't met Gage's standard. If so, had there been consequences? What had those consequences been? Had he and Gage's family been so fixated on Gage's side that they'd missed clues about the truth of Gage's marriage?

Darius closed his eyes, but when the image of Isobel's face, filled with sadness, hurt and resignation, just before she left the study, flashed across the back of his lids, he opened them again.

Nothing could excuse breaking one's marriage vows. But if her dreams had been crushed, if her marriage had been less than what she'd expected, if her husband had changed, was that why she'd turned to other men? Had she been seeking the affection and kindness she believed her husband hadn't given her?

Darius longed to ask her, because these questions tortured him.

"Darry!" Aiden shrieked, jerking Darius from his dark jumble of thoughts. Catching sight of him, Aiden scrambled out of Isobel's lap and dashed on his little legs toward him.

Joy unlike anything he'd ever experienced burst in his chest as he scooped the boy up and held him close. His heart constricted so hard, so tight, his sternum ached. But it was a good hurt. And not just because Aiden had thrown himself at Darius with the kind of confidence that showed he knew he would be caught.

But also because, for a moment, Aiden's garbled version of his name sounded entirely too close to *Daddy*. And as selfish as it might be, he yearned to be Aiden's father. Already he fiercely loved this boy as if they shared the same blood and DNA.

He kissed Aiden's still-warm forehead. "How's he feeling this morning?" he asked Isobel.

For the first time since he'd entered the room, she met his gaze. He noted the wariness reflected in her eyes. Noted and shared it. He might have been knocked on his ass by her confession the previous night, but he still didn't—couldn't—trust her. No matter how much his body craved hers. Actually, that grinding need only cemented why he had to be cautious with her. He'd shown in the past he could be led around by his dick, and he would never be that foolish again. Especially with a woman who had already betrayed her vows of fidelity.

And that was the crux of the war waging inside him.

Though it was difficult to reconcile the materialistic gold digger with the woman he was living with—the doting, sacrificing mother, the proud fighter—loyalty came down to family.

They'd earned it.

Isobel hadn't.

"He's still running a small fever, but it's lower than yesterday, and he has more energy. As you can tell," she added dryly.

He nodded, poking Aiden in his rounded stomach and chuckling at the child's giggling and squirming.

Setting the boy on his feet, Darius straightened, finding Isobel's stare again.

"Can I see you downstairs for a moment?"

"Fine," she said after a brief hesitation, rising from the floor and setting Aiden's book on his bed.

"I'll wait for you in the living room." Not waiting for her response, he retraced his earlier path down the hallway and staircase. He'd purposefully chosen the living room. Right now the study contained too many memories.

Minutes later, Isobel entered the room, and though he resented his reaction to her, his blood sang and his pulse drummed, the throb echoing in his cock. This was what she did to him by simply breathing. How did he armor himself against her?

God forbid she discovered his weakness.

"You wanted to see me," she said.

"Yes." He picked up a manila envelope from the mantel over the fireplace and offered it to her.

Frowning, she strode forward and gingerly accepted it. "What is this?"

"Open it, Isobel."

Flicking him a glance, she reluctantly acquiesced. He studied her as she withdrew the thin sheaf of papers and scanned the contract and bank documents. Bewilderment, shock and finally anger flitted across her face in rapid-fire succession. Her head snapped up, and her eyes narrowed. She pinned him with a glare.

"What. Is. This?" she repeated, her tone as hard as stone.

"Exactly what it looks like," he replied evenly, unsurprised by her response. "An addendum to our original contract. For entering our agreement, you receive one million dollars that will be deposited in an account under your name alone, as the bank documents reflect. It's yours free and clear. Even if you seek a divorce, it will still be yours."

"Like a signing bonus?" she drawled, the words acerbic.

He dipped his head. "If that's what you want to call it."

"No." She dropped the papers and the envelope on the glass table next to them as if they burned her fingers. "Hell no."

"Isobel—"

But she slashed a hand through the air, cutting off his explanation. "Is this about last night?" She shook her head so hard, her hair swung over her shoulders. "I didn't tell you that to make you feel guilty. If you hadn't pushed me, I wouldn't have said anything. At. All. But I damn sure won't take pity money from you now. If you wanted me to have that money—" she jabbed a finger in the direction of the papers "—then you would've included it during our original *negotiations*."

"You're right," he growled, and from her silence, he surmised his admission shocked her. "But at the time, I didn't want to hear anything except a yes. But now I want you to have it. And I can't unhear your fears or your dreams." Or the other things hinted at but left unsaid. "Maybe I need to give you what you missed. Your education. A father for your son. Help raising him. Time with him. Let me try to give it back to you, Isobel."

The only time in his life that he'd ever begged anyone for anything was when he'd pleaded with God to return his parents to him. But here, he came damn close.

She stared at him, and he battled the urge to turn away and evade that fey gaze that cut too deep and saw too much.

"Okay," she murmured.

He paused, her capitulation rendering him momentarily speechless. "Okay," he repeated. "And I'm not asking you to quit the supermarket or not replace it with something else. You can return to college, or I can arrange an entry-level position in a company or field of your choice that will allow you to get your foot in the door of your career. Or both college and the job. I don't want to steal your independence, Isobel. I don't want to be your jailor."

"Well, I really didn't want to ask my current manager for a reference anyway." A small smile flirted with her mouth. "Thank you, Darius."

"You're welcome," he said, his fingers suddenly tingling with the need to brush a caress over those sensual lips and feel that smile instead of just seeing it.

Silently, they stood there, snared in each other's gazes. She was the first to break the connection, and he bit back a demand for her to return to him, to give him her thoughts.

"I was going to bundle Aiden up and take him to see my mom. She's been calling nonstop since yesterday. I think she just needs to lay eyes on him." She halted, her eyes again meeting his. "Did you… I don't know if you'd like to…" Her voice tapered off, red staining the slashes of her cheekbones.

She was inviting him to come with her to visit her mother. Considering they didn't have a traditional relationship, introducing him to her family hadn't occurred. But she was offering that to him. It…humbled him.

"Why don't you invite her here instead since his fever isn't completely gone? I can send a car for her. Or go get her myself. Whichever she prefers. If you'd like, she can spend the day here with you and Aiden."

She blinked. "A-are you sure?" she stammered. "This is your home. You don't have to…"

"No, Isobel," he contradicted, injecting a thread of steel in the words. "This is our home. And it is always open to your mother, to your family."

She didn't agree with him—but she didn't refute him either.

And for today at least, it was a start.

Eleven

Isobel removed her earrings and dropped them into the old wooden jewelry box that had been a gift from her mom for her thirteenth birthday. Closing the lid, she picked up her brush and dragged it through her hair, meeting her own gaze in the mirror of the vanity. A smile curved her lips, and she didn't try to suppress it. Even if she looked like a dope wearing a silly grin for no reason.

Well, that wasn't true. She had a reason.

A wonderful day with her mom, Aiden…and Darius.

She carefully set the brush down as if it were crafted out of fragile glass instead of durable plastic. When truthfully, she was the one who felt delicate…breakable.

Inhaling a deep breath, she splayed her fingers low

on her belly in a vain attempt to stifle the chaotic flutter there.

Once the car bringing her mother had arrived, she'd expected Darius to retreat to his study or even head to his office. He'd done neither. Instead Darius had stayed with them, warmly welcoming her mother and melting her reserve toward him with his graciousness and obvious adoration of Aiden. They'd watched movies, played with Aiden, cooked, ate and laughed. She'd glimpsed another side of Darius that day. Charming. Relaxed.

Like his gift of the contract addendum and the bank account with more money than she'd ever see in five lifetimes. She shook her head. She still couldn't believe that. Not only had he handed it over to like it'd been change in a car ashtray, but he'd given it to *her*, the woman he considered a money-grubbing user. When she thought on it, the shock returned, and she had to stop herself from pinching her skin like some kid.

She could take care of Aiden.

She didn't have to work at the supermarket.

She could return to college.

She had no-strings-attached options.

A whirl of electric excitement crackled inside her. In the space of minutes, her world had expanded from the size of a cramped box to a space without walls, without ceilings.

He'd done that for her. For her son.

Isobel spun on her heel, charged out of the bedroom and marched down the hall before she could change her mind. Seconds later, she knocked on the door of

Darius's room. Already cracked, it swung further open under her hand.

"I'm sorry," she apologized, wincing as she shifted into the opening. "I didn't…know…it…"

The words dried up on her tongue, along with all the moisture in her mouth.

Good. Lord.

Darius stood in the middle of the room, naked to the waist. Miles and miles of golden, taut skin stretched over muscle like barely leashed power. Wide, brawny shoulders, strong arms roped with tendon and veins that seemed to pulse with vitality and strength. A solid chest smattered with dark brown hair that her fingers knew was springy to the touch. It thinned into a silky, sexy line that bisected his rock-hard stomach. Her gaze trailed that line, following it with complete fascination as it disappeared beneath the loosened belt and unbuttoned jeans.

Face heating, she jerked her head up, her stare crashing into his whiskey-colored one. Whiskey. Yes. She'd always compared it to an eagle's gaze, but whiskey was more accurate. Especially considering the punch it delivered and the heat it left behind.

"I'm sorry," she apologized again, inwardly cringing at her hoarse tone. Like sandpaper smoothed with jagged rock. "I didn't mean to interrupt…" She waved a hand up and down, encompassing his towering frame. "I'll just go," she said, already whirling around.

"Isobel." Her name halted her escape. No, it was the swell of arousal low in her belly that froze her. "Come here."

No "I'll meet you downstairs." Not "it's fine. Let me get changed and we'll talk later." Not even "come back." But, *come here*.

It was a warning. An invitation.

A threat. A seduction.

"Come here," he repeated, and she surrendered, her feet shifting forward, carrying the rest of her with them until she stood in front of him.

His heat, his cedar-and-musk scent, his almost tangible sensuality called out to her, enticed her to eliminate those scant few inches and bury her face against his chest. Inhale him *and* feel him. Somehow she resisted. But just. And even now that resistance was pockmarked, and so thin one touch would shred it.

"What do you want?" he asked, the sharp blades of his cheekbones and the hewn line of his jaw only emphasizing the blaze in his eyes. "Why did you come in here?"

"To thank you for today," she murmured. "For… everything."

"You're welcome," he rumbled, and as if in slow motion, he lifted a hand and rubbed the back of his fingers down her cheek. "Now tell me why you really came to find me."

She parted her lips to deliver a stinging reply, but it didn't come. Before she could contain it, the truth that she hadn't even acknowledged burst free.

"For you. I want you."

Another blast of flames in his eyes, and then her world tipped upside down. In one breath, she stood trembling before him, and in the next her back met his mattress, and Darius loomed over her. Her world narrowed to his big body and starkly beautiful face.

He tunneled his fingers through her hair, the blunt tips pressing against her skull. His gaze burned into hers, capturing her. Not that she wanted to be anywhere but here—his breath tangling with hers, his chest and legs covering hers, his cock branding her stomach through their clothes.

"Take it back," he ordered. When she stared up at him, confused, he lowered more of his weight onto her. She felt claimed. His flesh ground into her, teasing her with the promise of the pleasure only he was capable of delivering. "Take back your condition. Tell me you don't want me to fuck anyone else," he growled. "Tell me the thought of me touching another woman would drive you insane. Tell me I'm allowed to have you and only you."

She dug her nails into his shoulders, the words he demanded to hear crowding the back of her throat.

"Isobel," he growled.

The sexy, primal rumble unlocked her voice. "You can't touch another woman except me. You're not allowed, because it would drive me crazy," she finished on a gasp, with the word *crazy* barely out of her mouth before he swallowed it, his tongue thrusting forward past her parted lips and taking her in a kiss so blatantly carnal, so wild and possessive, it propelled the breath from her lungs.

But that was okay, because he gave her his.

He devoured her. It was wild, a clash, an erotic battle where both seized and neither lost. An ache opened wide in her, like a deep chasm that could never be filled. And yet she would never stop trying.

Did it register somewhere underneath the turbulent, consuming need that he hadn't asked her to make the same request? Yes. Did it also occur to her that he didn't ask because he didn't believe she would honor his demand of faithfulness? Yes. Did it hurt like a nagging, old wound? God, yes.

But right now, with his mouth working hers like he owned it, she didn't dwell on the pain. She submerged it beneath the waves of passion crashing over her. Later, when his hands didn't tilt her head back to receive more of him, that's when she'd think on it. But not now.

Darius abruptly straightened, tugging her up with him. With hurried hands, he balled the hem of her sleep shirt and yanked it over her head, leaving her clad only in a plain pair of black boy-short panties. Definitely not the expensive, seductive lingerie he was probably used to, but as he stared down at her, unchecked desire lighting his amber gaze, it didn't matter. Not when, without uttering a word, he told her he wanted her with a hunger that rivaled the need grinding her to dust.

Slipping a hand behind his neck, she drew his head down to her as she arched up to meet him. This time their kiss was slower, wetter. Somehow hotter.

He eased her back to the bed, his chest pressed to hers, and she undulated under him, rubbing her breasts over him, dragging her nipples across the solid wall of muscle. Correctly interpreting her message, he tore his mouth away from hers and blazed a path down her neck to the flesh that tightened in anticipation of his wicked attention.

As he cupped one breast, he nuzzled the other. She cradled his head, silently demanding he stop toying with her. And with a rumble that vibrated against her abdomen, he obeyed, parting his lips over her and drawing her in. She cried out, bowing so hard, her back lifted off the mattress. The strong pull of his mouth set off sparks behind her closed eyelids and matching spasms deep inside her. *God*, the ache. She wrapped her legs around his hips and ground against his cock, shuddering at the swell of pain-tinged pleasure. Whimpering, she repeated the action. Coupled with the mind-twisting things his mouth was doing to her breasts, she teetered close to the edge of release. So close…

"Not yet, sweetheart," he rasped against her skin.

Treating her nipple to one last kiss, he trailed his lips down her stomach, pausing to lap at her navel before continuing to the drenched center of her body. With an abrupt tug, he had her panties down her legs and tossed behind him.

Mortification didn't have time to sink its sharp nails in her as he lodged himself between her thighs, which were perched on his shoulders. She didn't have the opportunity to inform him that she'd never cared for oral sex, had never understood the allure of it. Didn't have a chance to tell him she'd just rather have him inside her because she didn't want to disappoint him.

No, she didn't say any of that because the second his mouth opened over her sex, shock and searing pleasure robbed her of the ability to think, to form coherent sentences.

"Oh, God," was all she could squeeze out of her constricted throat. He stroked a path through her folds, lapping at her, his growl humming against her. Grasping his head, she fisted his hair, to hold on and to keep him right there. He circled her clit, blowing on the pulsing knot of nerves, then he tortured her with short stabs and long sweeps. She writhed against his worshipping lips. Bucked into each stroke. Begged him to suck harder, faster, slower and gentler. She went wild.

And when release rushed forward in a flood so strong, so sharp, so potent, she didn't fight it. She surrendered to the undertow with a loud, piercing cry, chanting his name like an invocation.

Dimly, she registered the mattress dipping. Heard the soft shush of clothing over skin. Caught the crinkle of foil. Didn't have enough energy to turn her head and investigate. But when Darius reappeared over her, his big, beautiful body crouched over her like the gorgeous animal he was, desire rekindled in her veins, burning away the post-orgasm lassitude. It was unbelievable. She'd just come hard enough to see stars, and now, when it should've been impossible, her sex trembled and clenched, an emptiness deep inside her begging to be filled.

She lifted her arms to him, and without hesitation, he came down over her, one hand curving behind her head and the other cupping the back of her thigh, holding her open. With her eyes locked on to his, she waited, her breath trapped in her throat. Even when he pushed forward, penetrating her, stretching her, she didn't look away. The inexplicable but no less desperate need to see his face, his eyes, gripped her. She longed to see if they reflected the same awe, rapture and relief that surged within her. To determine if she was alone on this tumultuous ride.

His full, sensual lips firmed into a line. His nostrils flared, the skin across his cheekbones tightened and in the golden brown depths of his eyes…there, she saw it. The flare of surprise, then the blazing hungry heat and something shadowed, something…more.

No, she wasn't alone. Not in the least.

Wrapping her arms tighter around his neck, she burrowed her face in the strong column, throwing herself into the ecstasy, the burn, the passion—into him. Opening her mouth over his skin, she tasted his tangy, musky flavor, mewling as he burrowed so deep inside her, she wondered how far he would go, how much he would take.

Not enough. The answer quivered in her mind. *It won't ever be enough.*

A trill of alarm sliced through her, but it was almost immediately drowned out by the carnal havoc he created within her body. After sliding his hands down her back, he palmed her behind and held her for his long strokes. He forged a path that only he could travel, dragging his thick length in and out of her and igniting tremors with each thrust. She savored each one, rolling up to meet each plunge.

"With me, sweetheart," he murmured in her ear. Tunneling his fingers into her hair, he gripped the strands and tugged her head back. His eyes so dark with lust that only flickers of gold remained, he grated through clenched teeth, “I’m not going alone. Get there and come with me.”

The words, so arrogant and commanding, but strained with lust and drenched in need, were like a caress over her flesh. Clawing at his back, she slammed her hips against his, and his cock rubbed against a place high inside her, forming a catalyst, a detonator to her pleasure.

She shattered.

Screaming, she threw her head back against the pillows, propelling herself into the orgasm that claimed her like a ravenous beast, devouring her, leaving nothing. Above her, Darius rode her through it, until he stiffened and quaked. The throbbing of his flesh triggered another orgasm, rolling into the previous one like an unending explosion of ecstasy.

Darkness swept over her, pulling her under, but not before a seed of worry sprouted deep in her head. In the heat of passion, they’d become something new tonight.

But what? *Who?*

And would they survive it?

Twelve

Darius stared at his computer monitor, but he didn't see the report on the possible acquisition. Too many other thoughts crowded his mind. No, he had to be honest with himself.

Isobel.

Isobel crowded his mind, not leaving room for anything else.

Who was this woman? The selfish, devious conniver he'd believed her to be these past years? Or the woman he'd come to know since the night of the blackout? Just a week ago, he would've said both. That maybe single motherhood and being on her own had matured her from the person she'd been. But now…

Now doubts niggled at the back of his mind; perhaps he'd been wrong all along.

The things Isobel had hinted at—the controlling nature of her marriage, the lack of independence, the chameleon nature of the man Darius had called friend and she'd called husband—as well as the things she'd left unsaid. Working at a neighborhood grocery store even though she resided in one of the wealthiest zip codes in the state.

But if he believed Isobel—and God help him, he was starting to—then that meant Gage had concealed a side of himself from his family. What else had he hidden? Was it possible that Darius's best friend could've lied to them, to him? And if so, how could he have been so blind? He couldn't have been…right?

The urge to unearth the truth swelled within him, and he reached for the phone. He could have the company PI investigate for him. Contact Gage and Isobel's old neighbors or employees that had worked with Isobel at the time. It'd been years, but maybe they could give him some insight…

Just as his fingers curled around the receiver, the desk speaker crackled, and his executive assistant's voice addressed him.

"Mr. King, Mrs. Wells is here to see you."

Darius pressed the intercom button. "Thank you, Charlene," he replied. "Please let the marketing team know we're going to move our one o'clock meeting to one thirty."

"Yes, sir."

Darius rose from his chair and was already halfway across his spacious office when Helena opened his door and strode in. In spite of his unsettled thoughts, pleasure bloomed inside him at the unexpected but welcome visit. Several weeks had passed since the disastrous dinner at her home. Since then, he'd visited them several times, but without Isobel and Aiden. Though they'd asked about the boy and when they could spend time with him, Darius hesitated. First, he'd promised from the beginning that he wouldn't make arbitrary decisions about Aiden without consulting Isobel. And that included taking him to see his grandparents without her permission, even if he longed for them all to build a loving relationship.

Helena, regal in a black dress that wrapped around her still-slender figure, met him with outstretched arms.

"What brings you here today?" He led her to his office sitting area, lightly clasping her elbow.

She arched a dark, elegant eyebrow. "Do I need a reason to come see family? Especially when he's been a bit of a stranger lately?"

Darius laughed as he helped her settle on the black leather couch and then took a seat beside her. "That was subtle," he drawled. "Like a claw hammer to the head."

She smiled, but her point was well-taken. True, he hadn't been by the Wellses' home as often as he'd visited in the past. In the past weeks, he, Isobel and Aiden had settled into a cautious but peaceful routine. A truce that included Isobel in his bed, where they fucked until neither could move. God, she stripped him of his control, and that both terrified and thrilled him. Intimidated him and freed him.

It was the terror and intimidation that kept his mouth sealed shut when she slipped out of his bed in the dark, early mornings, returning to her room and leaving him alone. She never slept the night through with him. That bothered and relieved him.

Relieved him because the intimacy of sharing a bed smacked of a relationship, a vulnerability he wasn't ready to reveal to her. He'd given that trust to one woman, and she'd screwed him, literally and figuratively.

Bothered him because her sneaking out like he was her dirty secret didn't sit well with him.

"So you're here because you miss me?" he teased, deliberately dismissing his disquieting thoughts.

Helena's smile dimmed just a fraction, taking on a faintly rueful tinge. "Of course I do, darling. We all do. But I have another reason for coming to you. Next week is Thanksgiving. What are your plans?"

He stifled a sigh. Him joining them for the holidays was a tradition. But this year, it wasn't only him.

"I haven't discussed it with Isobel yet. She might want to spend the holiday with her family. And if that's her choice, I can come by the house afterward."

Anger flashed in her eyes, and she thinned her lips. "I see," she finally said. "You have a new family, whose wishes come first."

"Helena—"

"No." She sliced a hand through the air. "I'm glad you said that, it makes my next reason for being here easier to say." Her chin hiked up. "I want a DNA test for Aiden."

Shock whipped through him, and he stiffened under the blow of it. "What?"

"We want a DNA test," she repeated. "Yes, Aiden does resemble Gage, but that's not enough. In order for us to erase any doubt, we need to know he's Gage's son. And that can only be answered with a paternity test." Her features softened, and she settled a hand over his knee, squeezing lightly. "I need this, Darius."

His first reaction had been to flat-out refuse, but then reason crept in. Would having a DNA test done be so wrong? It would cement that Aiden was indeed Gage's son, and once the Wellses had the truth, they could finally lay this issue to rest and move on. He could give them that; he owed them that.

Isobel. He briefly closed his eyes.

Isobel wouldn't agree, just as she hadn't years ago. She would view it as an insult, but if it could facilitate healing... Yes, she would be angry about him going behind her back, but the results...how could she argue with the results when it meant the Wellses laying down their swords and Aiden having all of his family in his life, without doubts?

Meeting Helena's gaze, Darius nodded. "I'll arrange it."

Satisfaction flared in the blue depths. "Thank you, Darius. Another thing? Let's keep this between us for now. Baron doesn't know I'm here, and I don't want this impacting his health. So when you have the results, please contact me."

Unease over the further request for secrecy ate at him, but again he nodded.

"I should go," she murmured, standing. But then she hesitated, staring at him. "You're like a son to me, Darius," she said, steel entering her tone, belying the sentimental words. "And I love you, which is why I believe I have the right to say this to you. Gage fell for Isobel's sweet, innocent act, and look how he ended up. Betrayed, broken, angry…and dead. I would want to die myself if she did the same to you. So please, Darius, be careful, and don't succumb to the same game. Just…be aware, because Isobel is not who she pretends to be."

Darius didn't stop Helena as she left his office. After the door shut with a soft click, he slowly rose, her words of caution whirling inside his head.

Please be careful, and don't succumb to the same game... Isobel is not who she pretends to be.

He shook his head as if he could dislodge them, but they clung to him like burrs. Anger continued to dog him the rest of the day, nipping at him. He'd refused to play the fool again. But with Helena's warning ringing in his head, he couldn't shake the thought that her words had come a little too late.

Darius shoved open the front door to his house, the usual peace it brought him as he stepped into the foyer absent. His day had gone from hell to shit. By the time he left, hours earlier than his usual time, his employees had probably tossed confetti in the air as the elevator doors closed behind him. And if he were honest, he wouldn't blame them. His mood had been dark ever since Helena's impromptu visit, and even now, shutting the door behind him, he couldn't shake it loose.

He needed a drink. And time alone. Then, he mused,

heading toward his study, he'd go find Aiden and Isobel. It wouldn't be fair to inflict his attitude on them.

What the fuck?

He slammed to a halt in the doorway of the study, shock winding through him like frigid sleet.

Gage fell for her sweet, innocent act, and look how he ended up. Betrayed, broken, angry... Please be careful, and don't succumb to the same game... Isobel is not who she pretends to be.

As they had all day, Helena's words tripped through his brain, growing louder and louder with each pass.

Isobel sat on the couch in his study, with her head bent close to the man perched next to her.

On the same couch where she'd straddled him, and he'd pushed into her body for the first time.

Jealousy, ripe and blistering, ripped through him. The power of it rocked him, and it was only the unprecedented intensity that unlocked its grip on him. Dragging in a breath, he forced the destructive emotion under a sheet of ice.

As if she'd heard his deep inhale, her head lifted, and their eyes met.

Surprise rounded her eyes, and an instant later, a smile started to curve her mouth, but that stopped as she scanned Darius's face. It shifted into a frown, before smoothing into a carefully blank expression.

"Darius, I didn't hear you arrive," she finally said, voice neutral as she rose to her feet.

What did that expression hide?

Isobel is not who she pretends to be.

"Obviously," he drawled, then shifted his attention

to the tall man who now stood beside her. Handsome, wearing an expensive gray suit and about Darius's age. Green-tinged acid ate at his gut.

Faith used to wait until he'd left for the office, then sneak men into their house. Their bed had been a favorite location for her trysts. She'd gleefully thrown that information at him. Part of her pleasure had been in knowing that, at night, Darius would lie in the same bed where she'd fucked other men.

And here Isobel stood with some stranger. Playing the same game? After all, she hadn't expected him home from work this early. He studied her. Seeking signs of deceit, of guilt, but not expecting to find any. She was more of an expert than that.

"Where's Aiden?" he asked.

Translation: *Where is Aiden while you're down here...entertaining?*

From the narrowing of her eyes, she didn't require a translator. "He's upstairs, taking a nap. Ms. Jacobs is with him," she replied, tone flat. Turning to the man beside her, she waved a hand in Darius's direction. "Ken, let me introduce you to Darius King. Darius, Ken Warren."

"Nice to meet you, Mr. King," the other man greeted, striding forward with his hand outstretched. "Ms. Hughes speaks highly of you."

"Does she now?" he murmured, and after a pause in which he stared down at the extended palm, he clasped it. "A shame I can't say the same."

"Thank you, Ken," Isobel said, walking forward and shooting Darius a look that possessed a wealth of *fuck you.* "I appreciate you coming all the way out here. I bet house calls are rare in your profession."

"Not as much as you'd think." He chuckled. "Call me if you have any questions." Nodding at Darius, he said, "Again, nice to meet you."

She ushered him out of the room, and Darius moved into the study, stalking toward the bar. He poured Scotch into a glass and then downed it, welcoming the burn.

With his back to the door, he didn't see her reenter the room, but he felt it. The air seemed to shift, to shimmer like steam undulating off a hot sidewalk after a summer shower. That's how aware he was of her. He could sense the moment she entered a damn room.

Pivoting, he leaned a hip against the edge of the bar, taking another sip of the alcohol as he watched her approach.

"You are an asshole," she hissed, the anger she'd concealed in front of Ken Warren now on vivid display. It flushed her cheeks and glittered in her eyes like stars as she stalked to within inches of him. "I don't know what happened at the office, but you had no right to be so rude to him and to me. What the hell is wrong with you?"

"What's wrong is that I came home to find a strange man in my house, with my soon-to-be-wife, sitting on the same couch where I've fucked her," he drawled. "So forgive me if my mood is a little…off."

"I knew it," she murmured. For a long moment, she studied him as if trying to decipher a code that baffled her. "I *knew it*," she repeated, a soft scoff accompanying it. "I took one look at your face and could've written a transcript of your thoughts. *I caught her with her latest screw. In* my *house. I knew she wouldn't be able to keep her legs closed for long.* Am I close?" The sound that escaped her lips was a perversion of laughter. "You're so predictable, Darius."

She whipped around and stalked to the couch. Leaning over the arm, she picked up a small, dark brown box and marched back to him.

"Here." She thrust the case at him. "Ken is the husband of one of the moms I met at the Mommy Center Aiden and I go to on Tuesdays and Thursdays. When I found out he was a jeweler, I thought of you. Take it," she ordered, shoving the item at him again.

A slick, oily stain spread across his chest and crept up his throat as he accepted the box. As soon as he did, she moved backward, inserting space between them that yawned as wide as a chasm.

He clenched his jaw, locking down the need to reach for her and pull her back across that space. Instead he shifted his attention to the case. It sat in the middle of his palm. A jeweler. She'd said Ken Warren was a jeweler.

With his heart thudding dully against his sternum, he pried the top off. And it ceased beating at all as he stared down at the gold pocket watch nestled on a bed of black silk. A detailed rendering of a lion was etched on the face of it, the amber jewels of its eyes gleaming, its mouth stretched wide as if in midroar. Awed, he stroked a fingertip over the excellent craftsmanship and artistry.

It was…beautiful.

"When I saw it, I knew it was yours. A lion for both your first and last names. *Darius*, which means royalty, and then *King*," she murmured. "I thought it would be a perfect addition to your and your father's collection."

He tore his gaze away from the magnificent piece and met her eyes. Awe, gratefulness, regret and sadness—they all coalesced into a jumbled, thick mass that lodged in his throat, choking him.

She'd bought a gift for him, had chosen it with care and thoughtfulness.

And he'd returned that kindness with suspicion and scorn.

He'd fucked up.

"Thank you," he rasped. "Isobel…"

"Save it." She took another step back. "You're sorry now. Until the next time when I fail some test or, worse, pass it. Is this what I have to look forward to for however long this *agreement* lasts? I spent two years walking on eggshells. At least give me a handbook, Darius. Tell me now so I can avoid the condescending comments, the scathing glares and condemning silences."

"I'm sorry," he said, trying again to apologize. "You didn't deserve that."

"I know I didn't," she snapped. "But the truth is, you can say those two words, but you obviously believed I did. You convicted me without even offering me the benefit of the doubt. Of course, me sitting with a man couldn't be innocent. Not Isobel 'The Gold Digger' Hughes."

Suddenly the anger leaked from her face, from her body. Her shoulders sagged, and a heavy sadness shadowed her eyes. The sight of it squeezed his heart so hard, an ache bloomed across his chest.

"I just wanted to do something nice for you. To show you how much I appreciate all you've done for Aiden, show you all that you..." She trailed off, ducking her head briefly before lifting it. *Finish it*, he silently yelled. *Finish that sentence.* "I'm fighting a losing battle here, and Darius, I'm tired. Tired of trying to change your mind, of proving myself, of paying the price for a sin I never committed. I'm..." She shrugged, lifting her hands with the palms up in surrender. "Tired."

Slowly, she turned and headed toward the study entrance.

"Isobel," he called after her, her name scoring his throat. But she didn't pause, and desperation scratched him bloody, demanding he *stop her*. Give her the truth he'd kept from her. Pride and honesty waged a battle inside him. Self-preservation and vulnerability. "Stop. Please."

She'd jerked to a halt at his "please." Probably because she'd never heard him utter the word before. Still, her back remained to him, as if he had mere seconds before she bolted again.

Shoving a hand through his hair, he thrust the other in his pants pocket and paced to one of the walls of windows. "I don't remember you at the wedding, but you might recall that I married. Her name was Faith." He emitted a soft scoff. "When we first met, her name had seemed like a sign. Like fate or God sending me a message that she was the one. I'd wanted what my parents had, and I thought I'd found that with Faith.

"She'd reminded me of my mother. Not just beautiful and elegant, but full of life and laughter. Faith had a way of dragging a smile out of you even when everything had gone to hell. Dad used to call it the ability to 'charm the birds right out of the trees.'" In spite of the ugly tale he was about to divulge, a faint smile quirked a corner of his mouth. He couldn't count how many times his father had lovingly said that about his mom, usually after she'd used said charm to finagle something out of him. "Faith and I only dated several months, but the Wellses loved and approved of her, and I believed we would have a long, happy marriage… I was wrong."

Isobel's scent, delicate and feminine, drifted to him seconds before she appeared at his side. She didn't touch him but stood close enough that he could feel her.

"Within six months, I realized I'd made a mistake. The affectionate, witty woman I'd known turned catty, cold and spiteful. Especially if I said no to something she wanted. I discovered a little too late that she didn't love me as much as she loved what I could afford to give her. As much as the lifestyle I offered her." He clenched his jaw. The despair, disillusion and anger that had been his faithful companions back then returned, reminding him how foolish he'd been. "But even then, I'd still been determined to salvage our relationship. Hoping she'd change back into the woman I'd married. Then…" He paused, fisting his fingers inside his pants pockets. "Then I came home a day early from a business trip. Since it'd been late, I hadn't called to let her know I was arriving. I walked into our bedroom and found her. And one of my vice presidents. I froze. Stunned.

And in so much goddamn pain, I couldn't breathe. By this time, our marriage was hanging on by a thread, but I was still hopeful. Of all the things she could do—had done—I hadn't expected this betrayal. Didn't think she was capable of it."

Again, he paused, his chest constricting as the memories of that night bombarded him, the utter helplessness and grief that had grounded his feet in that bedroom doorway, rendering him an unwilling voyeur to his wife's infidelity.

A delicate hand slipped into his pants pocket and closed over his fist. He tore his sightless gaze away from the window and glanced at Isobel. She didn't face him, keeping her own stare focused ahead, but the late afternoon light reflected off the shiny track of tears sliding down her cheek.

She was crying.

For him.

Clearing his throat, he looked away, that tightness in his chest now a noose around his neck. He forced himself to continue. To lance the wound.

"I filed for divorce the next morning. We'd only been married a year and a half. A year and a half," he repeated. "I felt like a failure. Still do. I was so ashamed, I hid the truth from Baron, Helena and Gabriella. They still don't know why Faith and I divorced."

His admission echoed inside him like a clanging church bell. He'd never voiced those words aloud. Didn't want to admit that his disastrous marriage continued to affect his life years after it had ended. Thank God he hadn't been so lovestruck that he'd forgone a prenup.

He wouldn't have put it past Faith to try to clean him out just from spitefulness.

"Why?" Isobel asked, her voice gentle but strong. "You made a mistake. It doesn't make you a failure. Just human. Like all of us mortals. Wanting to believe in a person, wanting to believe in love, doesn't reflect on your intelligence or lack of it. It speaks volumes about your integrity, your honor, your heart. Just because that other person didn't have the character or dignity to respect their vows, to cherish and protect your heart, doesn't mean you're a fool or a disappointment. She didn't respect your relationship, you or herself. That's her sin, not yours. But, Darius," she turned to him, and he shifted his gaze back to her. "It's your decision, but you should forgive her, let it go."

He frowned. "I have forgiven her, and obviously I've moved on. I'm not pining for her." Hell no. That bridge had not only been burned, but the ashes spread.

"No, you haven't," she objected. "Forgiveness isn't just about cutting someone off or entering new relationships. It's deciding not to allow that person or that experience to shape your decisions, your life. It's not giving that person power over you even though they're long gone. And when your choices, your views, are influenced by past hurt, then those betrayals do have power over you." Her mouth twisted into a rueful smile. "I should know. I've fought this battle for two years. But understand—this is what I've had to come to grips with—forgiveness isn't saying what that person did was okay. It's just choosing to no longer let that poison kill you."

"Who have you forgiven, Isobel?" he murmured, but his mind already whispered the answer to him.

She didn't immediately answer, but seconds later she sighed and dipped her head in a small nod.

"Every day when I get up, I make the choice to forgive Gage. It's a daily process of letting go of the pain and anger. Especially since he's Aiden's father. I refuse to taint that for him with my own bitterness. And I refuse to be held hostage by it. Gage isn't here any longer. I'm never going to hear 'I'm sorry' from him. And even though Faith is very much alive, you most likely won't receive an apology from her either. So, what do we do? Forgive ourselves for the guilt and blame that isn't ours. But as long as we hold on to the past, we can never grab ahold of the future and all it has for us."

He stood still, her words sowing into his mind, his heart. By her definition, had he really released Faith, the past? He bowed his head, pinching the bridge of his nose.

"What about wisdom, Isobel? Only a fool or a masochist doesn't learn from his mistakes."

She slowly removed her hand from his and stepped back. He checked the urge to reach for her, to claim her touch again.

"Wisdom is applying those lessons, Darius. It isn't judging someone based on your own experiences. It isn't allowing the past to blind you to the reality even when it's staring you in the face." She lifted her hands, palms up. "Today you walked in here and jumped to the conclusion that I was sneaking behind your back with another man. That I had brought him into your home like your ex-wife. It's easier for you to be suspicious than to believe that maybe I'm not like her."

She inhaled and tilted her chin up, with defiance in the gesture, in the drawing back of her shoulders.

"I did not cheat on Gage, Darius. I never betrayed him—he betrayed me. He was the cheater, not me."

Before he could object, question her accusation or deny it—maybe all three—she pivoted on her heel and exited the room. Minutes passed, and when she returned, he remained standing where she'd left him, too stunned by her revelation. *Gage cheated? No. Impossible.* He'd loved Isobel. Hell, sometimes it'd seemed he'd loved her to the point of obsession. He couldn't, *wouldn't have*, taken another woman to his bed. Not the man Darius had known.

Did you really know him?

The insidious question crept into his brain, leaving behind an oily trail of dread and doubt.

"Here." She extended a cell phone to him. He reached for it before his brain sent the message to ask why. "It's my old phone, the one I had when I was married to Gage. I saved it for the pictures I'd taken of him for Aiden when he was older. But I want you to read this."

She pressed the screen and a stream of text messages filled the screen.

From Gage.

He tore his attention away from her solemn face to the phone.

I should divorce you. Where would you be then? Back in that dirty hole I found you. It's where you belong.

You'll never find someone better than me. No one would want you, anyway. I don't even know why I bother with you either. You're not good enough for me.

Don't bother waiting up for me. I'm fucking her tonight.

And below that message, a picture of Gage maliciously smiling into the camera, his arm wrapped around a woman.

Bile raced up from the pit of Darius's stomach, scorching a path to his throat. He choked on it, and on the rage surging through him like a tidal wave. Swamping him. Dragging him under.

She hadn't deserved the kind of malevolent vitriol contained in those texts. No woman did. And that his friend, one of the most honorable, kindest men he'd ever known, had sent them to his *wife*… The woman he'd proclaimed to love beyond reason…

Had Gage been that great of an actor? And to what end? The questions plagued him, drumming against his skull, not letting up. Because he needed answers. He needed to understand. His heart yearned to reject the idea that Gage could've been that spiteful…an abuser.

"Tell me," he rasped. "All of it."

After a long moment, her soft voice reached him.

"I was twenty when we met. And he was handsome, charming, funny and, yes, wealthy. I didn't—still don't—understand why he chose me. And I didn't care—I loved him. Becoming pregnant so soon after we married was a little scary, but seemed right. He'd started becoming a little moody and irritable a few months after we married, but soon after the baby arrived, and I refused the paternity test, he completely changed. I didn't understand then, but now I see he hated being poor, regretted being cut off from his family and blamed me for it. Resented me. That's when the isolation started. He needed to know where I went, who I was with. He decided my every move, from who I could spend time with to what I wore. Since I just wanted to please him, I gave in. But then I couldn't see my family because they were a 'bad influence.' And if I spoke to a man for too long, or smiled at one, I was cheating. The little money I earned, and the money his parents started giving him, he controlled that, as well. If I needed anything—from personal hygiene items to new clothes for Aiden—he bought them, because he couldn't trust me to spend wisely. I was trapped. A prisoner. And my husband was my warden."

"Why did you stay?" Darius asked, desperate to understand. To punch something. "Why didn't you leave?"

"Love," she murmured. "At first, love kept me there. I foolishly believed it could conquer all. But then that fairy tale ended, and fear and insecurity stepped in. I'd left school, had no degree. A minimum wage job. At that point, the unknown seemed far more terrifying than the known. And I never stopped believing that if I learned the proper way to act and speak, if I could get Gage to love me again like he used to, everything would be okay. His family would love and accept me, too." She shook her head, letting loose a hollow chuckle that bottomed out Darius's stomach. "And I wanted our child to have a two-parent home like I didn't. So I stayed longer than I should've. The night I told Gage I wanted a divorce is the night he..."

Grief tore through Darius. And, still clutching the phone with its offensive messages, he turned and stalked away from Isobel. His thigh clipped the edge of his desk, and he slammed his palms on the top of it, leaning all of his weight on his arms.

It was a death.

A death of his belief in a man he'd called brother. The demise of his view of him. Whom had Darius been defending all these years? How could he still love Gage...?

Her arms slid around him. Her cheek pressed to his back.

The comfort—the selfless comfort—nearly buckled his knees.

"It's okay to love him," she murmured, damn near reading his mind. Her voice vibrated through him, and he shivered in her embrace. "A part of me still does. For the memory of the man I initially fell in love with, for the father of my son. With time and distance, and loving Aiden, who is a part of Gage, I can't hate him. He was a man with faults, with issues and weaknesses. But he was also everything you remember him to be. A great, loyal friend. A loving son. A brother who would literally lay down his life for you. You can love those parts of him and dislike the parts that made him a horrible husband. There's no guilt or betrayal in that, Darius."

He pushed off the desk, spun around and grabbed her close, closing his arms around her. Crushing her to him. As if she were his lifeline. His absolution.

She clung to him just as tightly.

"I have a confession," she whispered against his chest.

"Yes?" he asked, the word scratching his raw throat.

"I never betrayed Gage, but…" She hesitated, tilted her head back. He lifted his gaze, meeting hers. She studied him for several long moments before dipping her head in a slight nod. "I noticed you, admired you. Somehow I instinctively knew you would never mistreat a woman. You were too honorable. And you've always been beautiful to me."

The soft admission reverberated in the room like a shout. He stared into her eyes—eyes that had captured his imagination and attention from the first glance.

"Sweetheart," he growled. It was all he got out before he cupped her face and crashed his mouth to hers. He couldn't stop, couldn't rein himself in if he'd wanted to.

And he didn't want to.

The avalanche of emotion that had eddied inside him burst free in a storm of passion and need so sharp, so hungry that fighting it would've been futile.

Her fingers curled around his wrists, holding on to him. Maybe designating him as her anchor as she, too, dove into the tempest. She leaned her head back, angled it and opened wider for him. Granting him permission to conquer, to claim more. More. Always more with her.

He dragged his mouth from hers, and turning with Isobel clasped to him, swiped an arm across the surface of his desk, sending books, folders, the cell and his home phone tumbling to the floor. After grabbing her by the waist, he hiked her onto the desk, follow ing her down. Covering her. Impatient, with a desperation he didn't want to acknowledge racing through him, he jerked her pants and underwear down her legs, baring her. Her trembling fingers already attacked his pants, undoing them while he removed his wallet and jerked a condom free. Within seconds, he sheathed himself and thrust inside her. His groan and her cry mingled, entwined together as tightly as their bodies.

And as they lost themselves in each other, as he buried himself in her over and over, he forgot about everything but the pleasure of this woman.

Of Isobel.

And for those moments, it was enough.

Thirteen

Isobel leaned closer to the vanity mirror, applying mascara to her lashes. When the doorbell rang, echoing through the house, she almost stabbed herself in the eye.

"Damn," she whispered, replacing the makeup wand.

It was Thanksgiving Day. Who could that possibly be?

She glanced at the clock on her dresser. One o'clock. A loud holiday meal with her mother, brothers and plethora of aunts, uncles and cousins was set for three o'clock at her mom's house. They were supposed to leave as soon as Darius returned from the store after a last-minute errand. For someone to show up uninvited on their doorstep on a holiday, it must be important.

Quickly rushing down the hall to Aiden's room, she leaned inside the doorway. "Ms. Jacobs, I'm going to get the door. But we should be ready to go in just a few."

The older woman smiled from where she played blocks with Aiden. "We're fine until then, Ms. Hughes."

"Isobel," she corrected, but the nanny just smiled and returned her attention to Aiden. Shaking her head and chuckling, she descended the steps. She'd been waging the war of getting Ms. Jacobs to call her Isobel, but to no avail. In the short time she'd known the woman, they had grown fond of each other. So much so, Ms. Jacobs was spending Thanksgiving with them since she didn't have children of her own.

It'd been Darius who had thought of that kindness.

Darius.

A spiral of warmth swirled through Isobel's chest, landing in her belly.

Ever since that evening a week ago, when he'd come home to find her with Ken and heard her full admission about Gage, a…connection had forged between them. One that, while tenuous, had her heart trembling with a cautious hope that what had started out as a marriage bargain between them might evolve into a real relationship. A relationship based on respect, admiration…trust.

Love.

The nervous snarls in her stomach loosened, bursting into flutters.

There'd been a time—not too long ago—when she wouldn't have believed herself capable of falling for another person. She hadn't thought she could ever take the risk of trusting someone with not just her heart, but with Aiden's.

But here, only weeks later, she stood on the crumbling precipice of a plunge into something powerful and dangerous—love.

And it was a beautiful, strong, loyal and fierce man who had her heart whispering with the need to take the fall.

She was afraid. Even as a fragile hope beat its wings inside her, she was *afraid.*

She reached the foyer and glanced out the window next to the door. Shock rocked through her.

Helena and Gabriella.

What…?

As if on autopilot, Isobel unlocked the door and opened it.

"Hello," she greeted, surprised at the calmness in her voice. "Please come in." As they passed by her and entered the house, she shut the door behind them. "Darius isn't here at the moment…"

"That's fine. We can wait," Helena said, turning to face Isobel with a coldly polite smile. "We apologize for showing up unannounced, but he told us you were having Thanksgiving dinner with your family. We wanted to catch him before you left."

Unease sidled through her veins, but she pasted a smile on her lips and waved a hand toward the living room. "He should be back shortly, if you'd like to wait for him in here."

Part of her wanted to run up the stairs and let Darius deal with his visitors when he returned, but at some point she had to become accustomed to being around them without Darius as a buffer. She could handle a few minutes.

"You and Darius seem to be getting along well," Helena commented as she moved into the room and settled on the couch.

Isobel nodded, stalling as she considered how to answer. As if a physical trap waited to be sprung at the end of her reply. "Darius is a kind man."

Gabriella strode over to the mantel and studied the array of pictures there. "Yes, he is. It's both a blessing and a curse," she said. "Have you two set a wedding date yet?"

Unease knotted Isobel's stomach, at both the cryptic comment and the switch in topic. "Not a definite date," she replied. But remembering the stipulations Darius had set in their contract, she added, "Sometime in January, I believe."

"You believe," Helena echoed, and Isobel couldn't miss the sneer in her words as her gaze flicked to Isobel's left hand. "No ring yet, I see. Doesn't that tell you something, Isobel?"

"No," Isobel murmured, sensing the shift in the other woman's demeanor and steeling herself. "But I suppose you have an idea about that."

"He hasn't set a wedding date and hasn't even bothered buying you a ring." Helena cocked her head, her steady contemplation condescending, pitying. "What you said earlier is very true. Darius is a good man. The kind who would sacrifice his own happiness for those he loves. Yet he's obviously reluctant to shackle himself to you. A man who is looking forward to marriage publicly claims his fiancée."

"I'm afraid she's correct, Isobel," Gabriella agreed,

strolling the few feet to stand next to the couch her mother perched on.

A smirk curved the younger woman's lips, and a sinking, dread-filled pit yawned wide in Isobel's chest. Was insulting her the purpose behind their visit? Or just a bonus since Darius wasn't home yet? She glanced toward the bottom of the staircase. *Please, God, let Ms. Jacobs keep Aiden upstairs.*

Briefly, she considered exiting the room. But that smacked too much of running, and she'd quit doing that when she returned to Chicago.

"You don't know anything about my relationship with Darius," she said, tone cool. "But why don't you go ahead and have your say so we can get all this out in the open? That way we no longer have to indulge in this pretense. You don't want me with Darius."

Helena's lips firmed into a flat, ugly line, anger glittering in her eyes. "I thought we were rid of you for good. But you found a way to sneak back in, didn't you? It wasn't enough that you used my son and took him away from us, but now you've latched onto my other son. And if we don't want to lose him or our grandson, we have to deal with *you*," she spat out.

"I would never come between you and Darius," Isobel objected.

"As if you could," Gabriella snapped. "We have a real relationship. We love each other. You don't know anything about that."

Dragging in a breath and struggling to contain her temper in the face of their venom, Isobel straightened her shoulders and tipped up her chin.

"As I was saying," Isobel gritted out. "I would never come between you and Darius. His relationship with you is yours. And if it's as strong as you say, then there's nothing I could do to harm it," she pointed out. Ignoring Helena's outraged gasp, Isobel continued, "But while you might revise history with Darius, don't look me in the eye and speak it to me. We both know I've never tried to keep you from your grandson. You were the ones who didn't believe he was a prestigious *Wells*." She uttered that name as if it were sour. "You decided he wasn't worthy of your time and attention. Your love. As for me, I don't need your approval or acceptance. I don't even want it. But now, for some reason, you've changed your mind, and I won't deprive Aiden of knowing his father's family. But if you believe for one second that I'll let you twist and poison him, then you're absolutely correct. You won't see him."

I won't allow you to turn him into his father.

"Twist him? Poison him?" Gabriella bit, her lips curling in a snarl. "That is rich coming from you of all people. You, a gold-digging wh—"

"What's going on here?"

All of them turned toward the living room entrance at the sound of Darius's voice. A steadily darkening frown creased his brow as he scanned Isobel's features before moving to Helena and Gabriella.

Relief coursed through her, but she locked her knees, refusing to betray any sign of weakness in front of the two women.

"Helena? Gabriella?" he pressed. "What are you doing here?"

Isobel desperately needed to retreat and regroup. Shore up her battered shields.

"They came by to see you. I'm just going to check on Aiden. I'll be right back." Forcing a smile that felt fake and brittle on her lips, she left without a backward glance at Helena and Gabriella.

"Isobel," Darius murmured, catching her arm in a gentle grasp as she passed him. "Sweetheart..."

"No, Darius," she said, slipping free of his hold. "Just give me a minute."

She left the room and prayed that when she returned, the two women he considered a surrogate mother and sister were gone. If not, she might not be responsible for her actions.

Fourteen

"What happened?" Darius demanded as soon as Isobel disappeared from sight. "And can one of you explain to me why I received a phone call from my nanny to return home as soon as possible because two women were attacking Isobel?"

Fury simmered beneath his skin. They both stared at him, their faces set in identical mutinous lines. Helena rose from the couch, turning fully to face him.

"Helena? Gabriella?" He strode farther into the room, halting across from them. "What. Happened? And don't tell me 'nothing' or 'everything is fine,' because both would be lies."

He'd glimpsed Isobel's face when he'd first entered the room. That cold, shuttered mask had relayed all he needed to know. She only wore that blank expression when hurt or angry. And from the shadows that had swirled in her eyes before she'd pulled away from him, both emotions had applied.

"I love you, Darius," Helena said, approaching him with her hands outstretched toward him. "You know I do. But how much longer is this supposed to go on? How much longer are we supposed to pretend that that...*woman* is welcome in our family?"

"Helena," he warned, his muscles tensing when she clutched his forearms.

He'd never pulled away from her touch before, but with those vicious words ringing in the room—no matter the pain they originated from—he couldn't take it. He stepped back, her arms dropping away. Hurt flashed across her face, her lips parting in surprise.

"Darius," Gabriella murmured, glancing at her mother, then back at him. A plea filled her gaze. "That's why we came here today. To tell you that we know you went through this farce of a relationship so we could have Aiden in our lives. You've sacrificed for us, but you don't have to anymore. Mother told me about the DNA test. And now that we have the results back—"

He slashed his hand through the air, dread spiking in his chest. "Did you tell Isobel about the DNA test?" he growled. Driving his fingers through his hair, he glanced away from the women. His motives—bringing closure to the family—had been pure, but Isobel would see it as a betrayal. He needed to talk to her first, to explain. "Gabriella, did you say anything to Isobel about the test?"

"No, I didn't say anything to your precious Isobel,"

she snapped, whipping around and pacing away from him. "But you should know that we've been talking and have come to some decisions."

The unease that had coiled inside him slowly unfurled. "What are you talking about?"

For a heartbeat, Helena and Gabriella didn't respond, just stared at him. The tension thickened until it seemed to suck all the air out of the room.

"Answer me," he grated out.

"Now that we know for certain that Aiden is Gage's son, we intend to go forward with the suit for sole custody," Helena announced. "We've already contacted our attorney."

"You. Did. Not," he snarled. Betrayal, rage and despair churned in his chest, and he fought not to hurl curses and accusations that would irrevocably damage his relationships with these people. "That wasn't my plan or my agreement with Isobel. The terms of which I expressly discussed with you."

Helena scoffed, waving a hand. "That was before we knew that Aiden was our grandson. *Ours*," she stressed, pressing a fist to her heart. "Gage would've wanted him raised with us. By *us* and not that…that deceiver, that liar. And no judge on this earth wouldn't see that we're much more fit parents than her."

"Darius, don't you see?" Gabriella implored, moving closer to him. She clutched his upper arm, and he curbed his automatic reaction to shake her off. And that reaction sent a blast of pain through him. "This is for you, too. Now you can break off this joke of an engagement. You did all this for us, and we love you for it. But now, with us suing for custody, you don't have to chain yourself to a woman you hate. We know you might not agree with this, but we believe it is for the best."

"For the best," he repeated. "Do you know all Isobel has been through with her marriage to Gage? He wasn't a loving, faithful husband. He emotionally beat her down, cheated on her. He mentally abused her. Now, after she survived that, you want to rip her child away from her."

"How dare you?" Helena hissed, anger mottling her skin. She advanced on him, eyes narrowed and glittering. "I love you like a son, Darius, but I won't allow you to speak ill of my son in this house. Who told you these lies that you're so willing to swallow? Isobel?" She spit the name, her mouth twisting into an ugly sneer. "So, you believe her over a man who you loved as a brother? Did she warp your mind? Is that it, Darius? Do you think you're in love with her?"

He parted his lips, but no words emerged. His pulse pounded in his ears, and his tongue suddenly seemed too thick for his mouth. Helena's question ricocheted off the walls of his skull.

Do you think you're in love with her? Do you think you're in love with her?

Over and over. *No*, his mind objected. *Not possible.*

He pivoted sharply on his heel and strode to the bank of windows. After Faith, he hadn't believed himself capable of having deep feelings for another woman. Just the idea of opening himself and risking that kind of pain once more… He'd vowed never to make himself vulnerable—*weak*—again. And Isobel…

She had the power to hurt him like Faith never did.

If he gave her the chance, and she betrayed him, she could wreck him.

The knowledge had fear and anger cascading through him. Could he take a chance? Could he crack himself open and lose not just his family—because the Wellses would view him as choosing her as the biggest betrayal—but also risk losing himself?

No.

Coward that he was, no, he couldn't risk it.

"Darius."

He jerked his head up, spinning around.

Isobel stood in the doorway. *How long had she been standing there? How much had she overheard?* He moved towards her, but she shifted backward.

And that one movement supplied the answers.

"Isobel, please let me explain."

She stared at him, numb. The blessed nothingness had assailed her from the moment she'd returned to the living room and overheard his conversation with Helena and Gabriella.

Did you tell Isobel about the DNA test?

We intend to go forth with the suit for sole custody.

No judge on this earth wouldn't see that we're much more fit parents than her.

Do you think you're in love with her?

That awful, damning silence.

The two women had left soon after she'd appeared in the room, but she hadn't moved. Hadn't been able to. And now, as pain invaded her body, she prayed for the return of the numbness.

"Yes," she agreed, voice hoarse. "You're right. Which should we talk about first? The violation of running a DNA test on my son behind my back? Or how *your family* intends to take my son away from me?"

He closed his eyes, and a spasm of emotion passed over his face. But it disappeared in the next instant.

"I'm sorry for not telling you about the DNA test, Isobel," he murmured.

"You're sorry for not telling me, but not for doing it," she clarified. A sarcastic chuckle escaped her. "You promised me we would make decisions regarding Aiden *together*. Without interference from the Wellses. You betrayed my trust."

"I didn't..." He broke off his sentence, briefly glancing away. "Yes, I did break that promise. And I'm sorry," he said, returning his gaze to her. "I am, Isobel. But my motives weren't to hurt or betray you. I thought if Baron, Helena and Gabriella knew for certain that Aiden was their grandson and nephew, he could bring healing to them. To this family. I wanted to give them that. But also, knowing you told the truth about him being Gage's would start to change their view of you, as well. Not only do they need to know their grandson and nephew—they need to begin to know you."

"No, Darius. Now they just think it was luck that Gage fathered him, out of all the other men I supposedly screwed." She shook her head. "But this isn't about them. It's about how you lied to me. It's about how you put them—their feelings, their welfare—above Aiden."

Above me. “And you handed them cause to take him away from me.”

“I won’t allow that to happen,” he growled, moving toward her, his arms outstretched. As if to touch her.

No. No way could she allow that. Not when she was so close to crumbling. She shifted backward, steeling herself against the glint of pain in his eyes.

“Agreeing to marry you, to move in here, to put my son under your protection was supposed to stop it from occurring. But it didn’t. I still find myself at their mercy. A place I vowed two years ago I would never be again. And all because I trusted you.”

“Do you really believe I would throw you to the wolves? That I would abandon you to face this alone? Do you think I’m capable of that?” he demanded, stalking forward, but he drew up several feet shy of her.

“Would you want to? No,” she whispered. “But would you do it all the same? Yes. If Baron, Helena and Gabriella made you choose between them and me, I have no illusions about whose side you would come down on. And I’m so tired of waging a losing battle between the past, your mistrust and Gage’s family. *Your family.* Because I’ll never be considered a member of that perfect unit.”

“That’s bullshit,” he snapped, his features darkening in anger. “We’ve been building something here. Something good. Our own place, our own family. You can’t deny that.”

She shook her head once more. Desperately needing space, she backpedaled, then caught herself midstep.

She was through running. Through letting others dictate her life, her truth.

"What we've 'been building' was founded on blackmail, lies and mistrust. It'll never be 'something good.'"

Raising her head, she committed every one of his features to memory. Though she might wish she could evict him from her heart, she never would.

That didn't mean she wouldn't try. She had to. For her peace. For her sanity. For her future.

"I love you, Darius," she admitted quietly.

His body stiffened, and lightning flashed in his eyes, brightening them so the gold almost eclipsed the dark brown. "Isobel," he rumbled.

"No." She slammed a hand up, though he hadn't moved toward her. "Let me finish. I didn't think I would ever be able to open my heart to another man. But you did the impossible. You made me trust again. Love again. Made me believe in second chances. And I thank you for that. And I might hate you for that," she whispered. "Because you showed me what happily-ever-after could be, then snatched it from me."

"Isobel," Darius rasped again, erasing the distance between them and cradling her cheek.

And for a moment, she cupped her hand over his, pressing his palm to her face and savoring his touch. But then she dragged his hand away from her.

"Do you love me?" she asked, staring into his eyes. Glimpsing the surprise flicker and then the shadows gather in them.

Darius stepped backward, a dark frown creasing his

brow. But he said nothing. And it was all the answer she needed.

"You awakened something in me," she said softly. "Something I wish would fall back asleep, because now that it's alive, I hurt. I…hope. The Isobel from two years ago would believe she could change you, make you accept her. Fight for her, if she just loved you hard enough. That Isobel would be happy with the parts of yourself you were willing to give her. But I'm not that woman anymore. I deserve to be a man's number one and to be loved and cherished and valued and protected. I deserve a man who will love me beyond reason, and though I'm not perfect, he will love me perfectly."

"What you want, I…" he trailed off.

The raw scrape of his voice and the sorrow in his gaze should've been a balm to her battered soul, but it did nothing.

"I'm not telling you this to emotionally blackmail you, Darius. I'm admitting this for *me*, not you. So when I walk out of here, I won't have regrets."

"Walk out of here?" he repeated on a low growl. His arms lifted again, but once more he dropped them, his fingers curling into fists. "We had an agreement. A contract. You can't just break it."

"We've been breaking the contract from the beginning. Becoming lovers. The DNA test. Falling in love with you." The contract was supposed to have been a defense against that. A reminder of who she was marrying and why. But it hadn't shielded her heart, just as Darius hadn't protected her and Aiden. "Do what you feel you need to do regarding the consequences. But I won't remain in this home, in this…arrangement knowing I can't trust you. That I will continue to pay the price for Gage's lies and the Wellses' grudges. I refuse to be someone's emotional and mental punching bag again. And every time you side with Gage's memory and his family, you deliver another blow. No, Aiden and I will be leaving today. But I won't keep him from you. He loves you, and I know you feel the same. We'll set up a schedule after we're settled…"

Her arms tingled with the need to throw themselves around him. Her throat ached with the longing to ask him to say something, to beg her not to go. To declare his love and loyalty.

But nothing came from him.

She straightened her shoulders and inhaled past the pain. Then she turned, exited the room and climbed the stairs. Once she entered her bedroom and shut the door, her back hit the wall and she slowly slid to the floor. The tears she'd been reining in fell unchecked down her cheeks. How long she sat there, quietly sobbing and hugging herself, she didn't know. But during that time, her resolve to do right by Aiden, and by herself, firmed until it resembled a thick, impenetrable wall.

She might be losing Darius, losing the future she'd so foolishly allowed herself to imagine for her and Aiden, but she was gaining more.

Her self-respect.

Her dignity.

Her.

And it was more than enough.

Fifteen

Darius stared down into the squat glass tumbler and the amber-colored bourbon filling it.

At what point would the alcohol send him tumbling into oblivion, where the memories from Thanksgiving couldn't follow? He'd been seeking the answer to this for four days now. But while he'd been fucked up, that sweet abyss of forgetfulness had eluded him. No matter how many bottles he'd gone through, he could still see Isobel's beautiful face etched with pain and fierce determination as she confessed she loved him—and then left him. Could still hear the catch in her voice as she accused him of betraying her trust. Could still hear the sound of the front door closing behind her and Aiden that afternoon.

Closing his eyes, he raised the glass to his lips and

gulped a mouthful of the expensive but completely useless liquid. But he was desperate to not just escape the mental torture of his last, devastating conversation with Isobel, but the terrible, deafening silence of his house. It'd chased him into his study, where he'd shut himself away. But there was no refuge from the emptiness, from the *nothing* that pervaded his home.

I deserve a man who will love me beyond reason, and though I'm not perfect, he will love me perfectly.

If Baron, Helena and Gabriella made you choose between them and me, I have no illusions about whose side you would come down on.

You betrayed my trust.

Do you love me?

Her words haunted him, lacerated him…indicted him.

But goddamn, he'd been crystal clear that he hadn't gone into this arrangement for love. He'd been more than upfront that he'd wanted to save the Wellses and her from an ugly custody battle. To protect Baron from any future health risks that a custody suit could inflict. To provide for Aiden. To unite the boy with his father's family. And everything he'd done—the engagement, the dinner with the Wellses, the DNA test—had been to work toward those ends.

He'd never lied. Never had a secret agenda.

He'd never asked for her love. Her trust.

When you let people in, they leave. He'd learned this lesson over and over again.

Isobel had left him.

Like his parents.

Like Faith.

Like Gage.

Anguish rose, and he bent under it like a tree conceding to the winds of a storm.

She'd begun to hope. Well, so had he.

In this dark, closed-off room, he could admit that to himself. Yes, he'd begun to hope that Isobel and Aiden could be his second chance at a family. But just when he'd had it within his grasp, he'd lost it. Again. Only this time… This time didn't compare to the pain of his marriage ending. As he'd suspected, Isobel had left a gaping, bleeding hole in his world. One that blotted out the past and only left his lonely, aching present.

A knock reverberated on his study door, and Darius jerked his head up. Before he could call out, the door opened, and Baron appeared. Surprise winged through Darius, and he frowned as the older man scanned the room, his gaze finally alighting on Darius behind his desk.

With a small nod, Baron entered, shutting the door behind him. Darius didn't rise from his seat as Baron crossed the room and lowered himself into the armchair in front of the desk.

"Darius," Baron quietly said, studying him. "We've been trying to contact you for the past few days, but you haven't answered or returned any of our calls. We've been worried, son."

The apologies and excuses tap-danced on his tongue, but after taking another sip of bourbon, "Isobel left. Her and Aiden. They left me," came out instead.

Baron grimaced, sympathy flickering in his eyes. "I'm sorry, son. I truly am."

"Really?" Darius demanded, emitting a razor-edged chuckle. "Isn't this what the plan was from the moment I announced my intentions to marry her? Trick her into complying with my proposal long enough to order a DNA test. And once the results were in, take her son and free me from her conniving clutches?" he drawled. "Well, you can tell Helena and Gabriella it worked. Congratulations."

He tipped his glass toward Baron in a mock salute before downing the remainder of the alcohol.

"I'm sorry we've hurt you, Darius. I truly am," Baron murmured. "Their actions might have been…heavy-handed, but their motives were good."

"Why are you here, Baron?" Darius asked, suddenly so weary he could barely keep his body from slumping in the chair. He didn't have the energy to defend Helena and Gabriella or listen to Baron do it.

Baron heaved a sigh that carried so much weight, Darius's attention sharpened. For the first time since the other man had entered the room, Darius took in the heavier lines that etched his handsome features, noted the tired slope of his shoulders.

Straightening in his chair, Darius battled back a surge of panic. "What's wrong? Are you feeling okay? Is it Helena? Gabrie—"

"No, no, we're fine." Baron waved off his concern with an abrupt shake of his head. "It's nothing like that. But I…" He faltered, rubbing his forehead. "Darius, I…"

"Baron," Darius pressed, leaning forward, bourbon

forgotten. Though his initial alarm had receded, concern still clogged his chest. "Tell me why you're here."

"This isn't easy for me to say because I'm afraid to lose you. But..." He briefly closed his eyes, and when he opened them, a plea darkened the brown depths. "I can't keep this secret any longer. Not when the reasons for keeping it are outweighed by the hurt it's inflicting."

The patience required not to grab Baron and shake the story from him taxed his control. Darius curled his fingers around the arm of his chair and waited.

"On Thanksgiving, you told Helena and Gabriella about Gage and Isobel's marriage. That he'd been cruel, abusive and faithless. Everything you said..." He dragged in an audible breath. "It was true. All of it. Their marriage was horrible, and Gage's jealousy, insecurity and weakness were to blame."

Shock slammed into Darius with an icy fist, rendering him frozen. He stared at Baron, speechless. But his mind whirred with questions.

How do you know? Why didn't you say anything to your wife and daughter?

How could you not say anything to me?

"How?" he rasped. "How do you know?"

Another of those heavy sighs, and Baron turned away, staring out the side window. As if unable to meet Darius's gaze.

"Gage told me," Baron whispered. "The night he died, he told me the truth."

"What?" Darius clenched the arms of his chair tighter. If they snapped off under the pressure, he wouldn't have been surprised.

Baron nodded, still not looking at him. "Yes, he found me in the library that evening and broke down, confessing everything to me. Isobel had demanded a divorce, and he'd been distraught. I'd barely understood him at first. But as he faced losing Isobel and Aiden, he'd come to me, horrified and ashamed."

Baron finally returned his attention to Darius, but the agony on the older man's face was almost too much to bear.

"My son… He was spoiled. Yes, he had a big heart, but Gage was entitled, and the blame for that rests on Helena's and my shoulders. He'd defied us by marrying Isobel but hadn't been prepared for the separation and disapproval from his family. Hadn't been ready to live on his own without our financial resources. But instead of faulting himself, he blamed Isobel. Yet he loved her and didn't want to let her go. So he'd alienated her from us physically and with his lies of mistreatment and infidelity. He admitted he lied about the cheating, but at some point he'd started to believe his own lies. Became bitter, resentful, jealous and controlling. It transformed him into someone he didn't know, someone he knew I wouldn't be proud of. Who he'd become wasn't the man I'd raised him to be. And I think that's why he confessed to me. His shame and guilt tore at him, and in the end it drove him out into the night, where he crashed his car and died." Baron swallowed, his voice hoarse, and moisture dampening his eyes. "Do I think Gage killed himself that night? No. I don't think it was intentional. But I also believe he was reckless and didn't care. He just wanted the pain to stop."

Air whistled in and out of Darius's rapidly rising and falling chest. A scream scored his throat, but he didn't have enough breath to release it. He squeezed his eyes shut, battling the sting that heralded tears. Tears for Isobel's senseless suffering at her husband's and family's hands. Tears for the man he'd loved and obviously hadn't known as well as he'd thought. Tears for the agony of conscience Gage succumbed to at the end.

"I'm sorry, Darius," Baron continued. "Sorry I lied to you, to Helena and Gabriella. Gage didn't ask me to keep the truth a secret, but I did because I couldn't bear causing them more pain on top of losing him. Even if keeping the secret meant standing by while Isobel was villainized. I made a choice between protecting his memory and protecting her, and now I realize my lie by omission is hurting not just my wife, daughter and Isobel, but *you*, a man I love as a second son. I can't continue to be silent. I can't allow her to be crucified when she's been guilty of nothing but falling in love with my son. Both of my sons."

Trembling, Darius shoved to his feet, his desk chair rolling back across the hardwood floor. He pressed his fists to the desktop, wrestling against the need to lash out, to rail over the injustice and torment they'd all inflicted on Isobel.

Stalking across the room, he tunneled his fingers through his hair, gripping the strands and pulling until tiny pinpricks of pain stung his scalp.

"You're going to tell Helena and Gabriella the truth," he demanded of Baron, who'd also stood, silently watching him.

"Yes," he murmured. "I planned on doing it today, but I felt you deserved to hear it first. Darius." Baron lifted his hands and spread them out in a plea of mercy, of surrender. "I'm so sorry."

"Sorry?" Darius laughed, the sound crackling and brittle with cold fury. "Sorry doesn't give her back the years where she was abandoned, left to raise a child on her own. If you knew Aiden was Gage's, why didn't you help her?"

"Gage said he believed Aiden was his, but I didn't know for sure. And she'd refused the paternity test, which deepened my doubts. And honestly, I hated her after Gage's death. I wanted her to suffer because I no longer had my son. I didn't want any reminders of him around—and that included her and a baby that might or might not have been Gage's. It was selfish, spiteful. Yes, I know that now, and I don't know if I can forgive myself for it. Gage told me I'd raised him to be a better man. But I don't know if I did."

Darius clenched his jaw, choking on his vitriolic response.

Helena and Gabriella might not have known the truth, but their behavior toward Isobel since she'd reentered their lives had been spiteful, hurtful. So unlike the gracious, kind, affectionate women he'd known for over a decade.

And he'd excused it.

Which meant he'd condoned it, just as Baron had.

Grief and searing pain shredded him.

He'd told Isobel he would never leave her out to dry.

Throw her to the wolves. But he'd done it. He'd broken more than a contract. He'd shattered her trust, his word.

His concern had been about betraying the Wellses, when he'd ended up betraying and tearing apart the family he'd created, the family he'd longed for—with Isobel and Aiden. The roar he'd been trying to dam up rolled out of him on a rough, raw growl. Every moment they'd shared since the night of the blackout bombarded him.

Laughing together in the hallway.

Sharing the stories of his parents' death and Gage in the dark.

Touching her.

Her fiery defiance in her apartment.

Her surrendering to the incredible passion between them.

Her quiet dignity as she confessed about her marriage.

Her resolute pride as she admitted she loved him, but could, and would, live without him.

Jesus.

He slammed a fist against the wall, the impact singing up his arm and reverberating in his chest. He'd marched into her apartment, self-righteous and commanding, accusing her of being deceptive and manipulative, when he'd been guilty of both to maneuver her into doing what he wanted. He'd entered their agreement acting the martyr. When in truth she'd been unjustly persecuted. It'd been he who'd entered their relationship without clean hands or a pure heart.

She was the only one—out of all of them—who could claim both.

And he loved that purity of heart. Loved that spirit and bravery that had looked at all the odds stacked against her and plowed through them one by one. Loved the passion that had stealthily, without his knowledge, thawed and then healed the heart he'd believed frozen beyond redemption.

He loved her.

The admission should've knocked him on his ass. But it didn't. Instead it slid through him, warm and strong, like a spring nourishing a barren field.

He loved her.

Maybe he'd started falling from the moment she'd coaxed him out of his panic attack with talk of movies and Ryan Reynolds. No doubt he'd fought his feelings for her, but if he were brutally honest with himself, the inevitable had occurred when she'd embraced him and assured him his love for his friend—her abusive husband—wasn't wrong.

A weight that had been pressing down on his shoulders lifted, and he could breathe. He could suck in his first lungful of air unencumbered by the past. Turning, he faced Baron. Darius loved him. But if it came down to a choice between him, Helena and Gabrielle, and Isobel and her son—*their son*—then Isobel and Aiden would win every time.

"I'm going to go find my family," Darius said.

His family. Isobel and Aiden.

From the slight flinch of Baron's broad shoulders, the emphasis hadn't been lost on him.

"I don't know what this means with you, Helena and Gabriella in the future. Maybe after you tell them the truth, they can find it in their hearts to forgive Gage and let the past go, including their hate of Isobel. But right now, that's not my issue—it's theirs and yours. If they can't, then we won't be a part of your lives. And that includes Aiden. I won't allow them to poison him, and you can inform them that if you continue in the pursuit of custody, I'll stand beside Isobel and fight you."

Darius pivoted and strode out of the study without a backward glance, steady and determined for the first time since Isobel and Aiden had left.

He had his family to win back.

If they'd have him.

Sixteen

Isobel pushed open the front entrance to her mother's apartment building, shivering as she stepped out into the cold December air. Her arms tightened around Aiden for a second before she set him on the ground.

"You're okay?" she asked, kneeling next to him and making sure his jacket was zipped to the top. "Warm?"

Aiden nodded as she tugged his hat lower. "See Darry?" he asked, his eyes wide, hopeful.

A dagger of pain slipped between her ribs at his expectant question. Just as it did every time he asked about Darius. Which was at least five times a day since they'd moved out of the house. At least. Aiden missed Darius, and to be honest, so did she. It'd been a long week. One where she forced herself not to dwell on him every minute of the day. She only succeeded a quarter of the time.

She smothered a sigh, shaking her head. "No, baby," she said, crying inside as his little face fell, the sparkle of excitement in his eyes dimming.

He didn't understand that they were no longer living with Darius, that he would no longer be a permanent part of their lives. And it crushed her to hurt and disappoint her son. Darius had called a few times, but as soon as she saw his number, she'd passed the phone to Aiden.

Hearing his voice, talking to him—she wasn't ready for it yet. Didn't believe she would still have the courage and determination to say no if he asked her to return home.

Home.

She'd constantly told Darius his house wasn't hers, but somewhere along the way, she'd started thinking of it as home. And she missed it. Missed Ms. Jacobs.

Missed him.

"See Darry," Aiden whined, tears pooling in his eyes. His bottom lip trembled.

She hugged her son tight, as if she could somehow squeeze his hurt and confusion away. "I know, baby. But right now we're going to see the lights and animals at the zoo, okay?"

She'd kept Aiden—and herself—busy with outings. They'd visited the Children's Museum at Navy Pier, the Christmas tree at Millennium Park and the model trains at Lincoln Park Conservatory. And now they were headed to Zoolights at Lincoln Park Zoo. Yet, during all the trips, she couldn't help but imagine how different they would be if Darius had been by her side. As a family.

Standing, she forced the thoughts away. Yes, she loved Darius. Maybe she always would. But he didn't return the feeling, and there was no getting past that.

They weren't a family.

"Good," she said, injecting cheer into her voice for Aiden's benefit. "Let's go—"

"Darry!" Aiden's scream burst in the air seconds before he yanked his hand out of hers and took off across the tiny courtyard.

"Aiden!" she yelled, but her footsteps faltered, then jerked to a complete stop as she took in the man stooping low to catch her son and toss him in the air before pulling him close for a hug.

And the love on that face as he cuddled Aiden… It stole what little breath her baby's mad dash away from her hadn't.

Darius.

Oh, God. Darius. *Here.*

Stunned, she watched as he kissed Aiden's cheek, grinning at whatever Aiden chattered about. Joy, sadness and anger filled her, and heat pulsed in her body at the sight of him. The wind flirted with his hair, and her fingers itched to take its place. Hair that just passed the five-o'clock shadow covered his jaw and emphasized the sensual fullness of his mouth. A long black, wool coat covered his powerful body. But she remembered in vivid and devastating detail what was beneath it. She craved the strength of it at night.

Darius shifted his attention away from Aiden and pinned her with that golden gaze. The intensity of it snapped her out of her paralysis. Still, her feet wouldn't move, and she stood, immobile, as he approached her, carrying her son in his arms.

"Isobel," he said, and she worked not to reveal the shudder that coursed through her at the velvet sound of her name.

"What are you doing here?" she whispered. Damn it. Clearing her throat, she tried again. "What are you doing here, Darius?"

Sighing, he lowered Aiden to the ground, and turning, pointed in the direction of the curb where his town car idled. "Aiden, look who came to see you."

The window lowered, and Ms. Jacobs popped her head out, waving to him. Shrieking, he ran to the car, and the older woman opened the door, scooping him up. In spite of the emotional maelstrom whirling inside her, Isobel smiled. Aiden had asked about her only slightly less than he had asked about Darius.

Rising, Darius slid his hands into his coat pockets. "I hope you don't mind. I didn't want him to overhear our conversation."

"No. He's missed her," she admitted softly. Shifting her gaze from the ecstatic pair back to him, she murmured. "You, too."

Darius nodded, studying her face as if he, too, were cataloging any changes that had taken place in the last week. "You look tired," he observed in a gentle tone.

She hardened her heart against his concern, shielding herself against the tenderness that immediately sprang to life. "What are you doing here, Darius?" she repeated her question.

"To see Aiden. And you," he said, his eyes gleaming. "I've missed you both. I just needed to lay eyes on you." Then he loosed a short bark of laughter that fell somewhere between self-deprecating and rueful. "That's not quite the truth. I came to find you and beg you to come back home. To give me—give us—a second chance."

Beg you to come back home.

The words echoed in her head and her chest, and swirled in her belly. A yearning swelled so high, so strong, that it nearly drowned out the steely resolve to not give in. She wanted to—God, she wanted to just walk into his arms and have him hold her.

But she couldn't live a life without love, acceptance, trust and loyalty.

She refused to settle anymore.

"Darius, we can't," she murmured, but he clasped her hand, and the *goodness* of his touch cut her off. But just as quickly as he'd reached for her, he released her.

"Please, sweetheart. I know I don't have the right—don't deserve the right—to ask you to hear me out. But I am." He paused, as if gathering his thoughts, then continued. "Everything you said to me was true. I betrayed your trust. I betrayed you. Our family. And I do mean *our family*, Isobel. Because that's who you and Aiden are to me. You two are who I look forward to coming home to when I leave the office. And that's who you are for me, Isobel—home. All these years I believed the memories of my time there with my parents made it that. But I forgot the reason I love the house so much is because it means family. It means love. And I didn't realize what was missing until you and Aiden came to live with me. The moment you left, it was empty, a shell. And I need you to come back, to return it to my haven, my sanctuary."

Her heart thudded against her chest, her pulse deafening in her ears. Hope—that stubborn, foolish hope—tried to grow. But she shut it down. Only more pain led down any road hope traveled.

"I can't…" She shook her head. "Darius, I know you love Aiden. And we…we…" God, she couldn't get it out.

"We burned together, Isobel," he supplied, and her breath snagged in her throat. "But that's not all that was between us. Is still between us. Before I knew who you were, I trusted you with things I hadn't spoken to another living soul in years. I didn't need to see your face to tell you were special, loving, kind and compassionate. You didn't change, Isobel. I did. I turned on you. I allowed the past with Faith and Gage to warp what my heart acknowledged all along."

He shifted closer, but still didn't reach for her. But his gaze… It roamed her face, and she shivered as if his fingertips had brushed her skin.

And inside…oh, inside she couldn't battle hope anymore. It broke through her shields and flowed into her chest, filling her.

"I love you, Isobel." He raised his arms, and after a moment's hesitation, he cupped her face between his palms. "I love you," he whispered. "Remember when I told you about my fear of the dark and falling asleep in our burning building?" She nodded, his tender clasp, his soft words rendering her speechless. "I didn't tell you everything. I believe I heard my mother and father shout my name, and that's what woke me up. I know how insane it sounds, but even from where they were, they saved me. And now I think it's not just because they loved me, but because they knew what waited for me. You and Aiden.

"I've waited for you. And I hate that I almost threw away our future, *us*. Sweetheart," he murmured, sweeping his thumb over her cheekbone. "I promise I'll never place anyone else above you and our son and any more children we have together. But if I've hurt you too badly and you can't give me your heart and trust right now, I understand. Know this—I'll still provide for you and Aiden until I can convince you to forgive me. Because, sweetheart, my heart *is* yours. And I refuse to give up on us ever again. I'll love you perfectly."

He'd gifted her with her own words. She blinked, trying to hold back the tears, but they slipped free. And he pressed his lips to her cheek, kissing them away.

"Talk to me, sweetheart. I need to hear your beautiful voice. You're the only thing keeping me sane," he whispered, his voice carrying her back to that dark hallway where they'd first connected. Where she'd started to fall for him.

Where they'd begun.

"I love you." She circled his wrists and held on to him. "I love you so much."

He crushed his mouth to hers, taking and giving. Savoring and feasting. Loving and worshipping. And she surrendered it all to him, while claiming him.

"Sweetheart," he said against her lips, scattering

kisses to her mouth, her jaw, her chin. “Tell me again. Please.”

“I love you.” Throwing her arms around his neck, she jumped, and he caught her, his hands cradling her thighs. Laughing, she tipped her head back, happiness a bird catching the wind and soaring free. “Now take us home.”

Epilogue

Six months later

Isobel groaned through a smile. "This is your fault. And you're going to deal with the fallout."

Beside her, Darius snorted, laughter gathering in his chest and rolling up his throat. "Do you want to go over there and tell him to leave the bouncy castle?"

She scoffed. "And face World War Three *and* Four? God, no." She elbowed him in the side. "I thought we had a conversation about this party, though. Low-key. Nothing too big or grand."

Darius scanned their backyard, where they were holding Aiden's third birthday party. The aforementioned bouncy castle claimed a place of honor right in the middle of the lawn, surrounded by a petting farm, a huge slide, games, face painting, clowns… Their place could double for a carnival.

He shrugged. What could he say? Having missed Aiden's previous two birthdays, he'd really wanted to handle this one. So, he might have gone a little…overboard. Still, as Aiden's high-pitched laughter reached Darius, he had zero regrets.

"Well, he is having a blast," Darius noted, watching their son slide down the "drawbridge" of the castle. "And look on the bright side. At least the party is out here, so in case of a blackout, no one can get trapped inside. With all these animals."

She laughed. "True." Smiling, she slid an arm around his waist and leaned her head against his shoulder. "He'll never forget this. All of his family here to celebrate him." Including Isobel's mother and brothers. They mingled with the children and parents with ease, laughing and talking.

Well, not with Darius's family. Since Baron had confessed the truth to Helena and Gabriella, they'd dropped the custody suit. Discovering Gage's faults hadn't been easy on them, and even now, months later, they still struggled with the magnitude of his lies. And his death. Though he knew Isobel held sympathy for them, relations between her and the Wellses had been put on hold. It would take a while to heal years' worth of pain, and Darius refused to push that reconciliation. Isobel had to move forward when she was ready, and until then Darius had her back. At least she'd allowed Aiden to see them, but only if Darius was there to supervise. And he would never betray her trust again.

It'd been six months since he'd gone to Isobel to plead for her forgiveness and love. Six months since she'd given him both, plus her trust, her heart and her body. She'd given him his family back. That had been the happiest day of his life. And the days that followed were just as wonderful, filled with laughter and joy.

She'd been accepted into the University of Illinois and was majoring in psychology to become a domestic-violence counselor. He wholeheartedly supported her. Isobel was living proof that a person could emerge from a destructive situation stronger, whole, and with the ability to find happiness and peace.

"And just think," Darius said, sliding behind her and settling his hands over the small bump under her tank top. "In another five months, we'll have another one to spoil. A girl. Just imagine the princesses and unicorns that will be prancing around here in another two years."

Isobel groaned, but it ended on a full-out laugh. The joy in it flowed over him.

"Thank you," he murmured, pressing a kiss under her ear. And when she tipped her head back, he placed another kiss on her generous, lovely mouth. "Thank you for filling my life with love and family. I love you."

Her grin softened, and she lifted an arm, cupping the back of his neck. "I love you, too. Always and forever."

"Always and forever."

* * * * *

The Chicago blackout trapped more than one couple in the mansion! What happens when the formidable Gideon Knight finds pleasure with a mysterious woman in the dark and then loses her in the morning?

Find out in the next Blackout Billionaires novel, available September 2019!

Only from Naima Simone and Harlequin Desire!

COMING NEXT MONTH FROM

Available July 1, 2019

#2671 MARRIED IN NAME ONLY

Texas Cattleman's Club: Houston • by Jules Bennett

Facing an explosive revelation about her real father, Paisley Morgan has no one to turn to except her ex, wealthy investigator Lucas Ford. Lucas has one condition for doing business with the woman who unceremoniously dumped him, though—a marriage of convenience to settle the score!

#2672 RED HOT RANCHER

by Maureen Child

Five years ago, Emma Williams left home for dreams of Hollywood—right before rancher Caden Hale could propose. Now she's back, older and wiser—and with a baby! Will the newly wealthy cowboy want a rematch?

#2673 SEDUCED BY SECOND CHANCES

Dynasties: Secrets of the A-List • by Reese Ryan

Singer-songwriter Jessica Humphrey is on the brink of fame when a performance brings her face-to-face with the one man she's always desired but could never have—her sister's ex, Gideon Johns. Will their unstoppable passion be her downfall? Or can she have it all?

#2674 ONE NIGHT, WHITE LIES

The Bachelor Pact • by Jessica Lemmon

When Reid Singleton buys the beautiful stranger a drink, he doesn't realize she's actually his best friend's little sister, Drew Fleming—until after he sleeps with her! Will their fledgling relationship survive...as even bigger family secrets threaten to derail everything?

#2675 A CINDERELLA SEDUCTION

The Eden Empire • by Karen Booth

Newly minted heiress Emma Stewart is desperate to be part of the powerful family she never knew. But when she realizes her very own Prince Charming comes from a rival family set on taking hers down, the stakes of seduction couldn't get higher...

#2676 A TANGLED ENGAGEMENT

Takeover Tycoons • by Tessa Radley

Hard-driving fashion executives Jay Black and Georgia Kinnear often butt heads. But Jay won't just stand by and let her controlling father marry her off to another man—especially when Jay has his own plan to make her his fake fiancée!

When Reid Singleton buys the beautiful stranger a drink, he doesn't realize she's actually his best friend's little sister, Drew Fleming—until after he sleeps with her! Will their fledgling relationship survive...as even bigger family secrets threaten to derail everything?

Read on for a sneak peek at
One Night, White Lies
by Jessica Lemmon!

London-born Reid Singleton didn't know a damn thing about women's shoes. So when he became transfixed by a pair on the dance floor, fashion wasn't his dominating thought.

They were pink, but somehow also metallic, with long Grecian-style straps crisscrossing delicate, gorgeous ankles. He curled his scotch to his chest and backed into the shadows, content to watch the woman who owned those ankles for a bit.

From those pinkish metallic spikes, the picture only improved. He followed the straps to perfectly rounded calves and the outline of tantalizing thighs lost in a skirt that moved when she did. The cream-colored skirt led to a sparkling gold top. Her shoulders were slight, the swells of her breasts snagging his attention for a beat, and her hair fell in curls over those small shoulders. Dark hair with a touch of mahogany, or maybe rich cherry. Not quite red, but with a notable amount of warmth.

HDEXP0619

He sipped from his glass, again taking in the skirt, both flirty and fun in equal measures. A guy could get lost in there. Get lost in her.

An inviting thought, indeed.

The brunette spun around, her skirt swirling, her smile a seemingly permanent feature. She was lively and vivid, and even in her muted gold-and-cream ensemble, somehow the brightest color in the room. A man approached her, and Reid promptly lost his smile, a strange feeling of propriety rolling over him and causing him to bristle.

The suited man was average height with a receding hairline. He was on the skinny side, but the vision in gold simply smiled up at him, dazzling the man like she'd cast a spell. When she shook her head in dismissal and the man ducked his head and moved on, relief swamped Reid, but he still didn't approach her.

Careful was the only way to proceed, or so instinct told him. She was open but somehow skittish, in an outfit he couldn't take his eyes from. He hadn't been in a rush to approach the goddess like some of the other men in the room.

Reid had already decided to carefully choose his moment, but as she made eye contact, he realized he wasn't going to have to approach her.

She was coming to him.

Happily-ever-after.
It's our promise,
whatever kind of love story you're seeking—
passionate, dramatic, suspenseful,
historical, inspirational...

With different lines to choose from
and new books in each one every month,
Harlequin has stories to satisfy even the most
voracious romance readers.

Find them in-store, online or subscribe to
the Reader Service!

SeriesIBC2018

In the dark, he kisses her...

Not knowing who she really is...

When a blackout hits Chicago, billionaire Darius King makes the most of it with an irresistible stranger. But then the lights reveal the woman in his arms is the woman he hates—his best friend's widow! His new plan: entice her into marriage to protect his friend's legacy. But wild attraction and explosive secrets could make that arrangement *very* inconvenient...

$5.25 U.S./$5.99 CAN.

CATEGORY
PASSION

ISBN-13: 978-1-335-60370-8

harlequin.com